Absolute Ambition

MEMORIA

David L Van Horne

ISBN: 099961570X
ISBN 13: 9780999615706

Volume I: Memoria

IN A PLACE and time very distant from here and now, a single planet was home to a chain of events that was destined to influence all of creation. Pearl, as it was called by its inhabitants, was a world that orbited a blue star near the heart of its galaxy. While the revolving rock was not extraordinary, the life that it cultivated proved to be the catalyst for the end of an era.

Decisions made by individuals who took part in this epic altered the basic fabric and laws of existence. A rip was torn across the universe, and time as well as space collapsed into nothingness. Reality was remade within this void, and those responsible were stitched into the elements of their conception.

This is a tale of an ending. It is a final chapter in circumstances that can now only be comprehended as fantasy. The rules of its physical aspects and the characteristics of its make-up are foreign to what is known today. Life, however, proves to be a common feature in most versions of existence. Beings creep and crawl out of the darkness without end. They multiply and evolve. As their complexity increases, their paths narrow.

Intelligence directs them into familiar territory, and their stories become relatable.

A fitting point to begin this saga would be on the continent of Setra. At the center of this large landmass, Pearl's capital, Urba, was dwarfed by a massive titanium plate that was assembled three hundred meters above the city by piecing together eight slices of metal. Each portion was supported by a stone pillar that was sculpted to resemble one of Pearl's eight holy trees.

The shadow that the plate cast over the city brought with it a myriad of problems, and the capital transformed beneath it. Urba split in two as some of its citizens migrated up and onto the artificial land. Megacorp's eight elevated vim reactors supplied stable, well-paying jobs to anyone who was lucky enough or well-connected enough to secure an available position. And so, local opposition to the company's efforts was kept in check by those who harbored hope.

High-priced properties and upscale retail outlets were threaded between and around the reactors. The opportunities presented by the plate beckoned ambitious individuals to compete with one another, and those who were hired felt their pockets grow heavy with shill. As the intelligent and motivated people ascended, the city beneath the plate devolved into the slums of the capital. Within the constant twilight remained shadowed citizens who lacked the desire and ability to improve themselves and their standard of living. Problems multiplied beneath the plate, and a cycle of degradation kicked in to gear.

Financial predators smelled desperation and scuttled into the shadows in search of an easy meal. Gangs and nefarious businesses traded monopolies as they sought to extract shill from individuals who could least afford to part with it. Those who dwelled beneath the plate felt their freedoms and liberty suffer as the trap of poverty slammed down upon them. Paralyzed by inability and slothfulness, many of them resigned themselves to a fate that was not of their choosing.

Eventually, crime and illicit trade became so rampant that the mayor of Urba claimed emergency political powers. He ignored objections from the city's legislators and secured military funding from the continent's chancellor. With the funds, soldiers from Megacorp's MERCENARY were hired to patrol the streets beneath the plate.

The MERCENARY soldiers became corrupted by the power that they were given. Ultimately, they caused as much grief as the drug traders and thieves that they had vanquished. Hardship seemed inescapable to anyone who called the slums home.

When the mayor was up for reelection, the vote split. The people who lived atop the plate believed that those beneath needed to be controlled by force, and so they supported the mayor and his heavy-handed tactics. The residents from the slums, however, thought that the ever-present soldiers were violating their rights, and they opposed the mayor's bid for reelection.

The result of the vote was close enough that the chancellor of the continent was charged with the task of creating a commission to fairly determine the winner. The controversy ended with the mayor being ousted by his rival. The MERCENARY soldiers were withdrawn, and crime began to rise again.

The residents of the lower half of Urba faced an insidious problem in addition to their socioeconomic woes. Although vim burned clean, the reactors required to cleanse and refine the energy spewed noxious fumes and radiation. Gaseous pollution was directed down into an underground network of pipes that led the toxins to neighboring sites that purified the pollutants.

This system, nevertheless, was imperfect. Leaks in the pipes allowed fumes to escape into the soil beneath the slums, and any remaining plant life withered and died beneath the eternal eclipse. This slow poisoning of the land spilled out from the center of the slums into nearby fields, farms, and villages.

Megacorp ignored objections from those who suffered. Shareholders wanted their investment to be as profitable as possible, and the company's executives accommodated their demands. Moral arguments were muted by the promise of financial gain, and innocents were forced to pay the price.

Megacorp's influence on the planet's capital increased once its plate was in place. If one event could be pinpointed as the moment when the public started to accept the company as something more than a business, it was when the democratically elected president of Pearl moved into an estate atop the plate. From then on, the citizens saw their government as Megacorp's partner.

The alliance between the company and Pearl's government was popularly regarded as a positive arrangement. The average citizen perceived the relationship between the two as natural.

Megacorp portrayed itself as a benevolent business that provided inexpensive energy and goods to the masses. This generated favor, and the company forged a dominating presence in the free market as well as the global government. Most of the people were nowhere near the slums, and few knew about the peril in the lower half of Urba.

Megacorp's eight elevated reactors supplied millions with power and dropped the company's energy prices for everyone on the planet. Eventually, the people became dependent on the benefits supplied by the plate, and the citizens of Urba restructured their city to suit it. Property lines were redrawn and the capital conformed to the slices of metal that comprised the plate.

Each portion of Urba was referred to as a division, and the divisions' borders were kept both on the plate and in the slums. The seemingly arbitrary act resulted in contrasts between the divisions. Competing factions arose, and a tier of prosperity segregated the poor from the poorer and the rich from the richer.

This story begins in the slums of Division Six. Garbage littered the streets, murder and robbery were common occurrences, and the people—the good people—were losing hope with each day that passed. Life suffered in that wretched place more than anywhere else on Pearl, but it persisted.

Despite their miserable circumstances, the people believed that somewhere, beyond the shadow of the plate, there was a place that made up for the hell that surrounded them. The legend of the Promised Land was what gave them the strength to keep going. Their faith in balance gave them confidence that there was always a light to vanquish the dark, a warmth to thaw the cold, and a good to counter the evil.

Chapter I

A SHRIEKING SOUND prevented Cirrus Stark from losing consciousness. Several hours had been spent repositioning himself on one of the orange chairs in the lobby of Division Six's train station. Despite his experience at passing out in public places, the incessant noise on this night was difficult to block from his inebriated mind.

The limitless independence of Cirrus's homelessness provided the young man with an ample amount of free time. He spent much of it riding the rails that snaked up, down, and around Urba before settling on Division Six's slum-level train station as his most frequented haunt. Its security was relaxed when compared with that of Urba's other train stations, and his vagrancy was able to continue unchecked.

His days were spent begging for spare shill in the train station's lobby, while his nights were spent sleeping in one of the smooth seats. He was able to collect enough of the metal cylinders to fund his drinking, but that was the extent of his success. Although his MERCENARY uniform allowed for a higher rate of shill to be thrown into his company hat, it never accumulated to a life-changing amount.

Cirrus refused to recognize the seriousness of his circumstances. He considered his homelessness as temporary and unavoidable. And he counted on a perpetually approaching but always absent recovery that he believed would push him forward onto the next stage of his life. This transitory period stretched as he cocooned himself within the gray.

After MERCENARY dropped him from its ranks, he was devastated. Being cut from the entry class was such a blow to his pride that he found the subsequent disappointment difficult to overcome. He was emotionally fragile, and his reality was blurred by self-pity and physical withdrawal.

The reasons for his departure from MERCENARY continued to weigh on his spirit, but his physical problems faded as time passed. His body, for the first time in a long time, was beginning to feel normal. This sentiment, however, was eclipsed by his despair.

Before being discharged from the Lindlamb MERCENARY medical center, his doctors informed him that depression would likely be one of the lasting side effects. There were drugs for the emotional imbalance, but he no longer benefited from the free medical treatment that was provided by the company. He was alone in a busy and unforgiving city, and the task of dealing with his misery verged on unbearable.

Megacorp faced such a surplus of willing recruits that their standards were high for all members of their military. Every year, a stream of youths joined MERCENARY. While all applicants were accepted, approximately eighty percent were weeded out of the entry class before too much shill was invested in them.

MERCENARY's standards were so high because no individual, faction or local government was willing to pay for an inadequate warrior. The soldiers who retained employment could count on exceptional fees for their services by ascending the ranks. This monetary incentive ensured the constant influx of recruits.

Before joining MERCENARY, Cirrus was confident in his ability to succeed within the organization. It was well known that not many from the entry class were kept, and he thoroughly prepared himself prior to his enlistment. Initially, his efforts paid off. Nevertheless, after his trials began, his edge dulled.

What followed the injections was beyond anything he expected. The foreign vim that was introduced into his body acted as a toxin. His physique weakened, and his perception warped. Confusion plagued his weary mind, and his subsequent actions tore through his sense of self. By the time his trials were over, what remained of the man was neither old nor new. Although many who underwent similar trials externally mutated, his change was internal.

For years, it had been Cirrus's dream to join Megacorp's military and reach the elite ranks of the first class. These celebrated soldiers received unmatched veneration. Villages expressed pride for their men and women who reached the upper echelons of MERCENARY, and he yearned to be one of the few citizens from Highwind to be recognized in a hero's light.

While he wished to be admired, he failed to garner much attention or praise throughout his adolescence. As is the case with most youths, his aspirations obscured the realities that were required to attain what he wanted. The blinders of ignorance and naiveté helped to preserve his far-off fantasies, and the cultivated bravery propelled him into the unkind world.

Having grown up without a father, Cirrus yearned for a male role model. As an adolescent, he began idolizing Aggeroth Wyvern. This exceptional MERCENARY soldier rose from obscurity and became renowned for his unmatched abilities. Aggeroth's life became a roadmap for success within Cirrus's mind, and he sought to emulate his idol. This led the young man down a path that he believed was necessary to achieve his goals.

And so, he dropped out of school and moved to Urba in his late teens with the intention of joining Megacorp's military. His mother opposed his decision, which resulted in them parting on bad terms. Wars and violence were a constant fact of life on Pearl, and she didn't want her son to die halfway around the globe.

As he matured, Cirrus found it difficult to muster emotions that could be considered the cornerstones of a balanced life. Although he harbored the same desires as all people, it was difficult for him to invest in anything or anyone. After his failure as a MERCENARY soldier, his persistent melancholy became more pronounced, and he slipped easily into the role of a nomadic street person.

His impending sobriety caused him to fidget sleeplessly on the frictionless chair as his sluggish mind drifted between memories of the past and the passing seconds. It was in this indefinite conscious state that he found himself thinking of the girl with the odd name. Sagacious was never far from his thoughts, but she tended to elude recollection. At this hour, however, her face and her voice emerged from what seemed to be nothing.

Cirrus and Sagacious had been neighbors while growing up in the small mountain town of Highwind. From the start, an inexplicable bond of understanding existed between the two. She was well liked by the children in their town, and Sagacious made it a point to include the otherwise solitary Cirrus into her social circle. In return, he appointed himself as her guardian. He defended her from the feeblest of threats and treated her with chivalrous respect.

The night before he left for Urba, he and Sagacious met at a nearby lake. Snowmelt from the mountains collected in the Emerald Mirror before it flowed south and away from Highwind. Webs of plant life stretched over and around the lake. Natural light was filtered into a soft glow that reflected from the water's surface. The river followed the path of least resistance and dwindled as it invaded the Amber Sands.

She wore a modest blue dress, which hid her blossoming body, while he sported a white shirt and a pair of cloth pants. Neither of them felt any need to impress the other. They dressed for comfort on that spring night.

Her pale legs dangled off the end of the pier. The bottoms of her bare feet glided above the chilly liquid. Rosa's ruddy glow strained through the plant life above their heads, and the golden illumination allowed for a bit of visibility.

He sat quietly next to her. The desire to say goodbye pressed upon him, but the proper approach eluded him. He knew that she recognized the purpose for this rendezvous, and neither of them desired to put into words their farewells.

Before he could summon the courage to speak, she asked him to make a promise. It was a simple and obscure request, and he didn't analyze it. He responded with a nod and returned his gaze to the yellow sparkles that flashed from the obsidian liquid.

The black water before his internal eye engulfed him, and he found himself floating in endless space. He suspected that he was moving at an incredible speed, but there was no way of understanding his progression. There were no objects, distant or close. He felt no resistance.

Nothingness began to absorb him, and upon realizing this, he found himself struggling to swim into it. Although constant noise surrounded his physical body, a sweet silence tempted him somewhere in the depths of his dream. Something was pulling him forward to an unseen destination, and he felt a desire not to arrive but to dissolve. The prospect, the idea, the possibility of becoming that which surrounded him stoked embers of desire.

Another train screeched to a stop not far from where Cirrus sat. The noise jerked him back to lucidity. His eyes peeked open, and the light that poured into him illuminated inescapable reality. He hugged himself as he attempted to evade consciousness.

Chapter 2

SAGACIOUS GARD WATCHED as the darkened scenery swept by her unmoving face. An unceasing hum whirred around and into her. The monotonous sound resulted in a shallow trance, and her unfocused mind wandered through several unrelated thoughts.

She turned her head from the window. Dash was busy scribbling notes and drawing crude maps of their target. His brow furrowed, and his actions paused. His white skin appeared more devoid of color than usual beneath the train's soft light. He lifted his free arm and ran his fingers over the red stubble that covered his head. His muscled limb's black tattoos contrasted with his fair complexion, and her focus shifted to the subject of his sketch.

Reality was beginning to dampen the rebel group's expectations. The chances of completing their undertaking dwindled as the facts emerged. The possibility of being killed tugged at her, and she grimaced.

Her gaze returned to the darkness. The train swept down from the surface of the plate as it rushed toward their destination. She pushed away the negative thoughts and tried to think of something else.

Her perspective lost itself in the blackness. The endless void before her allowed her thoughts to drift, and the image of her hometown's destruction formed within her mind. The reason for the pile of ash that was once Highwind remained unknown to her, and she strained her memories in an attempt to understand the past.

The devastation began with a fire at the Jecht estate. As it was the largest home in the town, the flaming edifice quickly drew the attention of many. A searing blast shot through the calm setting when Aggeroth Wyvern burst through the mansion's front doors. The accompanying explosion of fire and debris cast forth a wave of flames that engulfed the lush greenery that surrounded the property.

His lengthy silver hair danced in the breeze as he glided from the Jecht estate. His heavy black robe showed no indication of having been licked by flames. Its elegant fabric swung and shifted with his pace. If it weren't for his glowing green eyes, he would have appeared as he always had.

He proceeded to cut the townsfolk down with swift smooth stabs and slices. Others he incinerated with simple hand gestures. His movements were so quick that the commoners' eyes barely registered the lethal actions. None of them stood in his path for long.

It was from her bedroom window that Sagacious witnessed her father's death. With casual contempt, Aggeroth thrust his thin sword through her father's chest. From that moment on, she was responsible for herself.

As the ravenous flames devoured Highwind, Aggeroth set off on a path toward Mt. Terra. He strode at an even and unhurried pace. Small white stones crunched beneath his black boots as he passed the fields of tall grass and wildflowers.

With tears in her eyes and rage in her heart, Sagacious rushed from her bedroom and hurried down to the basement. She threw open the door to her family's storage room and rifled through the contents of an enormous chest. A spicy smell of the past sprung from the old wood and thick fabric. She tossed aside the trinkets and scraps of cloth that were collected to preserve fragments of the family's history.

The familiar sight of the Gard crest adorned a flat case at the bottom of the chest. Her shaking hands explored the sides of the case. Her fingers found its latches, and she forced the stubborn metal to unlock itself. Although little light reached the heirloom sword, it was enough to shine off the mirrorlike blade.

As she ran after her father's killer, tears streamed down her burning cheeks. The awkwardly placed battle belt around her waist caused the bulky sword to bounce off the white stones of the path. Her mind was silent, while her body acted. There was no plan—only a furious desire to drive the point of her family's sword into flesh.

After reaching the top of a hill, she spotted the two-story research center. A sprawling staircase spilled from the front of the building. Aggeroth's silver hair glimmered in Lazla's light and contrasted with his robe as he ascended the stone steps.

She rushed at him with the large weapon in her hands. Her bloodlust was her only preparation for the confrontation, and her unease was as apparent as her anger. Turning to face the source of the approaching footsteps, Aggeroth did not hesitate. His thin sword reappeared in a heartbeat. He thrust it into her side and shoved her down the unyielding stairs. She struck the white stones of the path, and pain overwhelmed her.

Her death would have been imminent, but as her warm blood pooled around her, a curative mystic swathed her in its healing glow. Her wound sealed within seconds. A hand reached to where the sword had struck her. There was no sign of damage. Shaken, she caught a glimpse of her childhood friend before she lost consciousness.

Sagacious sighed and attempted to examine the moving shadows. She hadn't thought of that day in years. Whether the vision of Cirrus standing over her was real or a hallucination remained unknown to her. Upon regaining consciousness, she found that her savior was gone, and she was left without an answer.

After burying her father, she left Highwind for Urba. She desired to be in a place as different from her hometown as possible. She wanted to shed the memories of that awful day. There was another reason for choosing the metropolis. She was searching for her childhood friend. She was searching for the boy who made her a promise and the man who kept it.

When she first moved to the capital city, she wanted to find him. Life, however, kept her from attempting to track him down. After her daughter was conceived, she began training in self-defense. She eventually became so skilled at hand-to-hand combat that she started teaching it. She dedicated her days to training other women, while her nights were devoted to her tavern. Cirrus became a distant but always beloved memory.

The train screeched to a stop. Sagacious looked to Dash. "You don't have to walk me home. I'll be fine."

Dash shoved his papers into his purse and met her gaze. "What if someone tries to mug you?" A smirk crept across his face.

"I'd like to see someone try. I've been working on a new move." She nodded to her right foot and twisted it to reveal its metal heel. "Picture this going through the skull of one of those *scary* muggers." She caught Dash running his eyes up her bare legs, and she redirected his gaze by waving a gloved palm in front of his face. "I can get back to Seventh Heaven all by myself."

He squeezed his way down the aisle of the train. "My father taught me to protect fair maidens from the creatures who live within the dark." His tone was jocular with an undercurrent of seriousness.

"If anyone needs protecting, it's you. Fighters might be powerful in the ring, but you guys are slower than tonbears. I know you think being the ninth best in your league is impressive, but it's not." She followed him into the cool darkness and watched as he clumsily stepped from the train to the landing.

Dash chuckled. "Where have you been? I'm eighth now!"

She hopped onto the solid ground. "Oh yeah? Who died?"

Dash feigned amusement and flicked her ear. "Why do you pick on me?"

"I guess I'm just a bully."

They made their way from the train to the lobby of the station. Soft light radiated from a tangled web of mesh that lined the high ceiling of the immense room. Owing to the time, the huge place was nearly empty. A few travelers strolled toward the doors or ticket counters, while others sat in orange chairs. With suitcases and bags at their sides, the people appeared weary and ready for bed.

Dash dropped his purse onto one of the chairs. "Hold up, Sagacious!" he shouted.

"Julie was expecting me back half an hour ago. Quit playing with your purse, and let's move!"

"I know we can handle trouble, but we shouldn't ask for it." He grabbed two pairs of metal knuckles and tossed the daintier set her way.

She smiled and slipped her weapon over her hands. "You're so—" she began.

"Sagacious?" A familiar voice came from behind her.

Chapter 3

EMMA STILLWATER STIRRED from her slumber as the bright light of Lazla made its way into her bedroom. Dust particles floated within the rays, and she stared into emptiness. One of her arms explored the bed. As her hand passed over nothing but fabric, gravity's pull felt as if it amplified. She couldn't do it. She couldn't go through it again. Every day, the discontent piled higher and higher, and it was beginning to crush her.

The house was too big. It felt hollow. The plan was to fill it with children, but Oryn and she had thus far been denied those blessings. He blamed her, she suspected. Was that why he agreed to the long-distance missions? Did he feel it too? The absence was like the specks that floated before her: ever-present and inescapable.

Somehow, she found the strength to pull herself up and out of the bed. Her gaze briefly touched on her bedroom's mirror, and the mess that was her brown hair caused her to pause. Her instinct was to run a comb through it, tame it, and make herself look presentable. But this notion vanished as quickly as it materialized. There was no point. Why go through the trouble?

She didn't go anywhere the previous day. She had no plans on this day.

Urba had been their home for some time, but it was still a foreign city. On the now rare occasions, when Oryn was in town, they spent most of their time together. When he was gone, she felt paralyzed. There was nowhere for her to go. There was no one to visit.

Oryn felt comfortable in this city. He insisted that they move there. He, like so many across Pearl, was drawn to the metropolis. Urba had always been the destination for youths who sought to break free of their humble destinies. Even before Megacorp had been unchallenged on all fronts, Urba was a city that offered opportunities to anyone who was willing to work hard for them.

After their wedding, he insisted on leaving Wynhill. He said it was too small for them. It was a beautiful place to grow up, but expectations did need to be tempered by its residents. She would've preferred to stay there, but she recognized his intense desire to grow beyond the simple life.

It was an unusual time for the planet. The energy revolution was changing everything at an incredible speed. Oryn loved the frenetic pace, but it terrified her. Before joining MERCENARY, his income had been unpredictable. He had taken whatever work he could find, while she tended her garden and kept the house in order. Several times, they were in danger of not being able to pay their bills, and it was she who insisted that he get steady work. An education was called for, but the only way he could afford one was via MERCENARY.

By joining the ranks, he was guaranteed a free pass through the University of Urba. And so, it was agreed that he would serve in Megacorp's army.

Through her kitchen window, Emma watched as a massive stone pillar was being shaped by a swarm of laser-wielding drones. They buzzed around it while shooting beams of light that caused pieces of it to break away. In a recent letter, Oryn explained that it would resemble the tree of Fates, but she doubted such beauty could be replicated.

The rapidly advancing technology was the primary reason for her self-seclusion. There was always a new electronic thing, and she had no interest in trying to keep up with all of it. Her weekly trips to the market reaffirmed her stance. Adults and teenagers walked around as they stared at hand-sized devices. Children fiddled with toys that spoke and played music. No one made eye contact.

Oryn tried to get her to use one of the devices. He told her it was a means of communication. Words were sent back and forth in an instant. But the thing, whatever it was called, remained dead in her dresser drawer. She preferred her words on paper, written with ink, and carried by men. He sent daily letters, and that was good enough for her.

As the hot water poured over the skillet, she scrubbed the food remnants off it. The chore only received a bit of her attention as she watched the distant scene unfold. Those flying machines looked like cotels from a distance, but they moved in swift, straight lines through the air. Their order seemed exactly coordinated with one another. The red light that they emitted cut through the stone, and the debris disintegrated as it fell to the soil.

All the gadgets that were popping into existence were powered by vim. She supposed this aspect explained how they were able to perform their mystic-like feats. Faith and religion had never much interested her, but the idea of using vim as a power source still felt wrong. There was surely a reason that essenia refused to be utilized in such a manner, she figured. For centuries, people had attempted to use the crystals as a source of mechanically drawn upon power, and each time their efforts ended in an explosion that destroyed the essenia and whatever contraption was around it.

Oryn's MERCENARY-issued essenia orb was the first she had ever seen. Before Megacorp, before the industrialization of essenia production, the crystals were nearly impossible to find. It took them many years to form. Vim churned itself beneath the planet's surface, and as it did so, bits drew upon one another and slowly the crystals grew. As they formed, they sank deeper and further out of man's reach.

There were legends as to what caused the particles of vim to draw upon one another. Emma believed that essenia crystals were individuals who reconstituted themselves after death. Surely, she thought, whatever force for good that created Pearl wouldn't allow the consciousnesses that it cultivated to vanish.

Her beliefs aside, she knew the facts. She knew one's vim, one's individuality, found its way into the ever-flowing, ever-growing vimstream upon death. But what of the memories? What of the personalities? Science gave no answers. It was assumed, by those who studied the subject, that one's vim was simply recycled within the vimstream.

As Emma strolled between the rows of plants, her eyes darted over the garden in search of pests. It was infested with tuggles this year. They were drawn by her kuple plants, and the furry critters stopped at nothing to get the berries that formed beneath the plants' blue flowers. If that wasn't bad enough, the tuggles were using her luash patch as a nesting ground. They bored holes in her luashes, kicked out the purple meat and red seeds, and used the thick rind of the large fruits to protect their fingernail-sized offspring.

She had tried putting up a fence but quickly learned that the tuggles had no trouble going under it. At the market, she overheard two women discussing their issues with the creatures. One of the women said that tuggles hated ghysal greens, and that if a garden was surrounded by the spindly plants, the tuggles would vacate the area. This proved to be partially false. The tuggles did seem to hate the ghysal greens, but they didn't leave her garden. The night after she planted the ghysal greens, the pests uprooted them and dragged them from her property. It took her two full days to clean up the mess.

Luckily, it seemed as if tuggles were territorial. The problem appeared to be capped at one set of them and their offspring. And since they were limited to their fill of kuple berries, she was left with whatever they couldn't eat. So, she kept a watchful eye on the blue flowers and trimmed them in an effort to sync their kuple berry production. This plan proved to be satisfactory. But it was a chore, and she was left with more than enough kuple berries every few weeks. She would've preferred a steadier supply and thus vowed to herself that she would chase away the tuggles if ever given the chance.

Her basket was overflowing with orange qweets and kuple berries when she spotted Irvin making his way toward her house. The board that carried him over the gravel road was new. Prior to that day, whenever he brought her letters from her husband, he came on his rolling board. It rattled him, going over the bumpy road, and the first time she noticed how it jarred him, she offered to pick up her mail from Megacorp's nearest office. But Irvin asked that she not. He wished to keep his job and feared the loss of demand.

His new board looked similar to his old one, but instead of rolling over the gravel road, it floated. His grip on the board's handle appeared to be tight, and his face looked thrilled but uneasy. On his back was a pack that was full of letters and packages. The corners of boxes poked at the pack's fabric, while the edges of envelopes stuck out from the barely closed mouth of it.

She passed through the short fence that separated her backyard from her front and waved to the boy. He smiled and returned the greeting. As he did so, the board began pivoting, and he quickly returned his freed hand to its place. The corrective action, however, overcompensated, and the board spun in a semicircle before Irvin lost his balance and fell to the unforgiving gravel.

She dropped her basket and ran the short distance that separated them. The wind threatened to lift her dress, and she struggled to restrain it without losing speed. She felt the mess that was her hair fly in multiple directions as her thin-soled slippers pressed against the gravel.

"Irvin!"

"Hi, Mrs. Stillwater." The boy looked up from his sitting position on the gravel. His hands encircled his right knee as blood oozed from it.

She gaped at the sight and looked around for help. She knew she wasn't strong enough to carry him anywhere. Oryn could do it, but—

"Are you okay?" Irvin asked.

The question surprised her, and she attempted to gather her thoughts. "You could've killed yourself on that thing!" she exclaimed.

His hands left his knee and he stood. "I'm fine, it happens. I'm still learning how to ride it. It's a lot different than my old board."

Blood dripped down his white skin, and she found it difficult to look elsewhere. "Come along, we need to clean that and cover it."

He shrugged and bent over to grab the board.

"You're not going to get on it again, are you?"

"Nah, not right now." He pushed a button on his transportation's handle, and the board began to fold in on itself. The place on which he had been standing became smaller than the handle, and it slipped into the bar that was connecting the two. He then turned two switches, one on each side of the handle, and this allowed him to fold the two sides of the handle over the bar. "My dad got it for me for my birthday. I really like it, but it's hard to ride."

She nodded and led the way. "Maybe you should stick to what you know."

"I wouldn't ever learn anything new though," he replied.

She looked back at him as she opened the door to her house. That response was too wise for someone so young. "That's a good point," she admitted.

"Yeah," he agreed.

He placed his pack and what was left of his board on the floor, near the Stillwaters' dining-room table, and sat while she disappeared down a hallway. His eyes wandered around the room and passed over the untended surfaces. Portraits of Mr. and Mrs. Stillwater lined the maroon walls of the large room. They appeared to be of the couple on their wedding day. Irvin noted that she looked a lot different in real life.

When she returned, her hands were filled with several different items. She awkwardly carried them to the table and allowed them to fall onto the dusty wood. "First, we need to clean it, and then we'll cover it with a wrap."

"Okay, can I have some heelo juice too?"

She looked up from the instruction label on the sanitizing solution. "What? Yes, of course, let's get this over with first." She unscrewed the cap and grabbed a pad off the table. When it was soaked with the solution, she looked to him. "Do you want me to do it?"

He shrugged.

"Okay, it's going to sting, so be prepared." She brought the wet pad to the bloody scrape and was sure to keep it on the wound when he jerked in response. Aside from an intake of breath, he remained silent. After a few seconds, she removed the pad and found herself questioning where to put it. With no better option, she placed it on the floor.

"When is Mr. Stillwater coming back?" he asked.

She picked at the wrap as she unwound a sufficient strip. "Oh, I'm sure it will be soon." She tore the piece from its source and started wrapping the injured leg. "Do you have a letter for me today?" she asked.

"Yeah."

After she was done tending to him, he began rifling through his pack. He pulled out an envelope and almost handed it to her but stopped and shoved it back in the pack. A few seconds passed as he shifted things around, until he smiled and pulled out another envelope. "Here it is," he announced.

"Thank you, Irvin. You may get the heelo juice," she mumbled. The envelope that he had handed her was a typical one. The hand-scrawled address label was neatly printed. She examined it more closely.

Irvin swooped down and grabbed the blood-soaked pad. "Thanks, Mrs. Stillwater." He ran into the kitchen.

Her hands ripped the envelope's thick paper, and she unfolded its contents.

Her eyes raced over the words once, twice, a third time. Her surroundings disappeared for a moment, and all she could see was the paper in her hands. Her mouth became a desert as she felt a tear drop to the floor.

"What's wrong?" Irvin asked. In one hand, he held a glass of pink juice.

She quickly folded the paper and held it close to her dress. "Nothing," she replied. A smile formed on her face. "Oryn is coming home soon."

Chapter 4

CIRRUS FELT THE blood drain from his face. The voice of the woman who passed by him, as if summoned by his earlier recollection, belonged to Sagacious. A large man with an intimidating presence was calling after her. It was the use of her uncommon name that confirmed his suspicion. His sky-blue eyes fluttered open, and he looked up.

Her chestnut hair was pulled back and behind her. It was held in place by a green band of fabric. She caught the two small items that the red-haired man threw in her direction and slipped the polished objects over her hands. Her stance and manner of speech projected her familiar, stalwart character.

She was a few years older, and she no longer seemed delicate. Her leg and arm muscles were apparent at first glance. She resembled a female MERCENARY soldier who might specialize in hand-to-hand combat. Her femininity, however, was not lost. Her natural beauty was still on display for the world to see.

As a boy, he regarded her as someone delicate and precious, and he charged himself with protecting her perfect form. His feelings were beyond the scope of attraction. Thus, he never tried to tarnish his perception of her by advancing their friendship.

She was standing roughly a meter from where he was seated. He wondered if she was real and questioned his consciousness.

He forced himself to his feet. His right arm shot to the back of his chair as he attempted to steady himself. The dim room spun around him while a cloud of black dots raced across his field of vision. He shook his head and blinked. His greasy blond hair wobbled out of place, and some of it fell over his forehead. With his free hand, he pushed it back up.

"Sagacious?" he asked.

With her hands on her hips, she turned around. Her smile faded as she recognized the unkempt man in front of her. "Cirrus…is that you?" She squinted in an attempt to see past the dirt and facial hair.

He recognized disgust briefly cross her face, and he dropped his gaze from hers. He regretted drawing her attention. "Yeah, it's me," he admitted.

"Uh, Sagacious?" the red-haired man asked. He stepped to her side as he crossed his thick arms. His light-brown eyes bore into the ex-MERCENARY soldier, and revulsion radiated from his powerful frame.

"This is Cirrus Stark. We grew up together." She raised a hand and forced her smile to come back. "We were next-door neighbors," she continued. She eyed Dash with the hope that he might end the awkward moment.

"I'm Dash Black." His tone was simultaneously cold and heated.

"Nice to meet you," Cirrus mumbled. He reluctantly stuck out a dirty hand.

"So, you're in MERCENARY then?" Dash asked. He ignored the briefly outstretched hand. "That's interesting, Sagacious. Your friend works for *Megacorp*."

"I'm glad that you were able to fulfill your dream," she said.

Dash smirked. "Your dream?"

The words came faster than Cirrus could comprehend. His hollow stomach sucked at his spine. Hunger and thirst had taken a backseat to his need for alcohol. His balance became his primary focus. "Thanks, but, uh, it didn't work out." He forcefully blinked. The spots again appeared in his field of vision. He swayed.

"Oh?" Her tone lifted.

"Yeah." His grip tightened on the back of his orange chair.

"But bro', you're wearing—" Dash began.

"Let it go!" she snapped.

Dash leaned toward her. "He doesn't look too good, and I'm not talking about the MERCENARY rags," he whispered.

The rocking became too much to handle, and Cirrus collapsed into his chair. Colors lost their sharpness, and his awareness faded. Nothingness engulfed him.

Sagacious kneeled near his chair. "Cirrus, are you okay?" Her voice trembled with worry. "What's wrong?"

"I'm no medic, but if I had to guess, I'd say he's had too much to drink," Dash said. "Can't you smell the booze on him?"

Her dark-chocolate eyes briefly glared up at Dash before returning to Cirrus. A spike of hair fell over one of Cirrus's eyebrows. She brushed it to the side and studied his appearance. Even in his current state, she found him beautiful.

When they were children, his chivalrous actions impressed her father. This combined with the boy's angelic face, calming blue eyes, and striking blond hair to draw her toward him. It was enough to convince the little girl that they were meant to be together.

Her crush waned as the years passed. His interest in her as anything other than a friend was clearly nonexistent. In their early teens, she accepted that their friendship would never evolve into anything more. This was confirmed by his openly pursuing others with no regard for her feelings. She was hurt by his insensitivity, but she never told him. It was better to have him as a friend than nothing at all.

"Okay," she breathed. "I'm going to need you to help me carry him back to my place."

Dash glowered at her. "He was in MERCENARY! I get that you two were friends, but for fuck's sake, he's still wearing the damn uniform." He clinched his jaw, and a vein protruded from the paper white skin of his neck. "And you do remember what we're up to, right? Our current situation doesn't exactly mix well with the likes of him." He kicked Cirrus's chair.

She turned to the wall of muscle. "I trust him. I know this might not be the best idea, but I can't just leave him here."

"What if he's still in contact with MERCENARY soldiers? What if he overhears something back at HQ? You have to think about Darlene. If we put aside the obvious reasons, bringing home a drunken bum still isn't the best parenting tactic."

"Oh please, I own a tavern! Darlene and I have lived beneath Seventh Heaven her entire life. In fact, I believe the first time you met her, you were stinking drunk. Remember, you asked to hold her, and I said no, and you started to cry—"

Dash held up his hands and glanced from side to side. "Hey, whoa, I did *not* cry."

"Like I said, I trust him. He has done more for me than I'd like to admit, and I want to help him if I can." She looked back to Cirrus's face.

One of Dash's dark-red eyebrows perked up. "Were you two an item back in Highwind?" he asked. "Were you schoolyard sweethearts? Your taste in men is—"

"If I were you, I wouldn't finish that thought. Now quit stalling, and give me your purse. I'll carry that while you carry him. Come on big man, let's put those muscles to work!"

Chapter 5

SAGACIOUS PULLED AN oversized key ring out of Dash's purse and unlocked the thick metal door of her tavern. The small structure was in the heart of the Division Seven slums. The neon-yellow sign above the entrance announced the establishment's name. It cast a soft glow that served as the street's sole source of light.

Shortly after she opened the tavern, Seventh Heaven became one of the few popular places to spend one's time in the Division Seven slums. Before establishing it, she had spent some time atop the plate in Division One, where she served drinks at a location near Reactor One. While working there, she gained the knowledge and experience required to run a business. After she became pregnant, she decided it was time to open her own place.

Establishing Seventh Heaven was difficult and required a large portion of her savings. But after her daughter was conceived, she refused to stay atop the plate. She found Megacorp employees and especially MERCENARY soldiers intolerable. It wasn't fear that she felt, but disgust. She didn't want to be reminded of the incident. She didn't want to associate the pregnancy or her child with it.

Although the situation was unexpected, she welcomed the baby. It was true that the little girl came in contact with more drunks than most toddlers, but Darlene was happy and loved by everyone in her life. The otherwise stoic patrons of the establishment were always glad to see the child. Some of the more sociable regulars would make it a point to interact with Sagacious's daughter while the ever-present mother kept a watchful eye.

The lock clicked open. "Tired?" she asked. Dash followed her into the dark.

"Are you kidding? He weighs nothing. I can't believe they'd let such a scrawny guy into MERCENARY."

"I'm pretty sure most of the specialties chosen by new soldiers are in artillery or swordsmanship. Neither skill requires much physical discipline or presence. Swordsmen are encouraged to be thin and nimble. He must have chosen that as his specialty." She flipped a switch, and the tavern's mesh slowly illuminated. A smile emerged as she noticed that Julie had cleaned up after her shift.

"Do I want to know how you know that?" Dash asked. He followed her to the tavern's backroom. The walls were lined with wooden boxes that contained every variety of liquor. Weak light reflected off the colored glass that peeked through the evenly spaced boards. At the center of the enclosed space, a lumpy sofa and a table sat across from each other. A spiral staircase, behind the couch, led down to Sagacious's apartment.

She removed her metal knuckles before setting them on the table. "I worked near Reactor One, remember? A lot of the clientele were MERCENARY soldiers and other Megacorp employees. The soldiers would try to impress the pretty maid by telling me tales of their *oh so* arduous training."

Dash dropped the subtly snoring Cirrus onto the couch. She unfolded a mauve-colored blanket from the sofa's back and gently covered the sleeping man. "The skinny ones are usually swordsmen," she explained. "Artillery experts are often out of shape, while the physically strong tend to be hand-to-hand specialists."

She lifted the blanket and pointed to Cirrus's clunky belt. At the center of a tarnished buckle, a transparent green orb rested. "All of them have at least one green essenia orb, and they're trained to use offensive mystics with it." She rearranged the blanket. "When he wakes up, you should ask him if he can show you how it works. I know you've always wanted to learn how to use essenia."

Dash shook his head and headed toward the spiral staircase. "I don't want to learn it that badly," he stated.

She rolled her eyes and followed him down the stairs. "He's a good guy," she responded.

Dash grunted.

At the bottom of the stairs, the petite Julie Dagger stood waiting. A near-permanent smile highlighted her beauty and contrasted with her odd and masculine fashion sense. Her garb consisted of a gray short-sleeved shirt over baggy sewage green pants. A blood-red headband pushed her unkempt hair back and out of her face. "How'd it go?" she asked. Even at this early hour, her excitement was palpable.

The distracted mother ignored the question. "Was Darlene good for you?" she asked. She swept across the living area and peeked into Darlene's dark bedroom. One of the little girl's arms was wrapped around a stuffed vaegah. Sagacious turned around and rejoined the others.

"Of course!" Julie answered. "She's always so much fun. After I opened Seventh Heaven, she was telling old man Galuf all about vaegahs, and how she's going to live on a farm with a whole bunch of them."

"She's fascinated by those gigantic cats," Sagacious mumbled. She walked into the kitchen. "I suppose we can thank uncle Dash for that obsession."

He and Julie followed her and settled themselves on stools near the countertop. "Hey, I took her to one race one time, and she had a blast," he interjected.

Sagacious grabbed a clear bottle of brown liquor and poured three shallow glasses before sitting down between her friends. "Well, now she wants a real one." She turned to Dash. "If you have any idea where we could put the stable, and how we could afford—"

"Guys!" Julie interrupted. She raised her hands to cover her smile. "Sorry, but I want to hear about how the recon went!"

Dash grabbed his glass and downed the bitter alcohol in one gulp. His face became rosy, and he exhaled through his nose. "We'll have to do it from the outside." He shook his head and put the glass on the countertop. "We could cause a lot more damage if we could somehow get inside, but the place is locked up tighter than a good girl's undergarments. We made it onto the site, but the reactor itself has only one conventional way of getting in. The upside is that there are just two MERCENARY soldiers guarding the reactor during the early hours of the morning. We might have a chance of getting in and setting off your bomb if we go during that window of time."

Julie took a swig from her glass. "We should just storm the place and somehow get to the core. Now, if my bomb goes off in a reactor's core, WAVE would definitely make a splash! There'd be a chain reaction, and we'd get a big boom!" She mimed an explosion with her hands.

"As much as I'd like for that to happen," Sagacious began, "I need to think about coming home." She glanced in the direction of Darlene's room. "I don't want this to be a suicide mission. It's a start. Tomorrow, before Lazla's first light, we'll bomb the scaffolding off Reactor Seven, if that's all we can manage to do. Brack and Wells seem pretty confident that they can manipulate Megacorp's network. After they arrest the site's hub, we'll do a brief broadcast from the location. By morning, everyone in Urba will know about WAVE's mission and purpose." She swirled the contents of her glass and stared at it. "Hopefully that'll lead to more recruits, and then maybe, someday, we can get that big boom."

After putting down the glass, her stomach tightened. A rustling of thick clothes sounded from the living area. She jumped off the stool.

Cirrus was in the middle of the living room. His bright blue eyes answered her immediate question. Her heart started to race.

Chapter 6

GALE STARK GRABBED the black orb from its place on her dresser and unlatched her necklace. Once the essenia was fixed between both sides of the silver web, she dropped it down her blouse and found her eyes in the mirror. She fought to keep a smile from growing on her face; the anticipation was difficult to keep under control.

The dim glow provided by her bedroom's candles was just enough to ready herself. Her curly, auburn hair looked perfect for once, and she hoped that the night's air would be accommodating. She found the thimble-sized glass on her dresser and dipped a finger into it. Crushed anzel bone clung to her skin, and she carefully brushed the shimmering white powder over her eyelids. A worrying thought emerged, and she yanked open a drawer. She grinned as she saw a single heelo berry roll toward her.

The small pink fruit wasn't firm, but she preferred the overly ripe darker shade. She pierced its thin skin and brought it to her bottom lip. Once a thick layer of the pink syrup was in place, she popped the deflated berry in her mouth and swallowed the sweetness. Her lips pressed together, and she rubbed them over each other.

She pulled a long strip of fabric from another drawer, and an aromatic scent rushed toward her. After wrapping the ends of the strip over her palms, she began rubbing the taut material between her thighs. After a few seconds, she tossed the strip aside and checked her appearance a last time in the mirror.

To keep her bedroom door from creaking, she opened it quickly. The cool air of the dark hallway sent a chill up her spine as she closed the door behind her. Very little was visible, but she wasn't worried. She took two short steps forward, then a long one leftward to avoid the creaking board. The snoring of her father made its way to her ears, and her breath stilled as she tiptoed by her parents' bedroom.

After descending the stairs, she shoved her feet into the attractive but uncomfortable shoes that she had carried with her. The front door's knob was half-turned when she heard heavy breathing behind her. She looked over her shoulder and met the excited stare of Beau. His three tails snapped straight and braided themselves in a blur.

"Go back to bed, Beau," she whispered.

He tilted his head, and his faintly glowing gray eyes enlarged. A whine emitted from his feather-covered neck, and his muzzle parted in preparation for a howl.

"No, Beau!" she hissed. "Go lay down. I'll be back soon, I promise."

The braided tail fell apart, and Beau's eyes shrank. His head dropped, and he slowly began pivoting away from her. A barely audible whimper made its way into the foyer.

"I'm sorry, we'll go on our walk later, okay? Just be quiet; I'll be back in a few hours."

Beau's muzzle parted again, and he pivoted back before licking her face. She fought to keep from reacting and patted his head. His eyes grew large again, and he spun away toward his bed. As soon as he was out of sight, she wiped away the saliva and exited her family's home. Rosa was large and full in the night's sky. The cool mountain air was still, and the relief that she felt fueled an exhilaration that drove her onward toward the Emerald Mirror.

Highwind was a small town. Gale knew everyone in it. She had lived there, in the same house, her entire life. Those, with whom she grew up, were like siblings. For nearly two decades, they had studied together, and now as they were entering adulthood, many of them were falling in love.

The boys who had teased her were now young men who were eager to become romantic with her. She already loved them, but the thought of being sexual with them felt almost incestuous. For years, she wanted her feelings to change, she wished for it, but they never did.

The red glow of Rosa became golden as she passed beneath the greenery that stretched over the Emerald Mirror. Beneath the living cave, silence greeted her. The soft soil's thin grass brushed against her ankles as she made her way toward the calm water. A pier stretched before her, and atop the aged wood, there he stood.

He didn't see her yet. His gaze was fixed off the end of the pier on the sparkles that reflected from the water. The blond hair that she would've killed for seemed to illuminate in the unique atmosphere, and she wondered how it was possible to feel such an attraction. This stranger, this man was so different from anyone in Highwind. He was fresh blood, imported from the big city. He smelled of train travel. His voice plucked an inner chord, and she wanted to envelope him.

"Hello, Gale."

Her slow pace came to a sudden stop. He was still staring into the water. Surprised by his lack of surprise, she scrambled for the right introduction. How should she present herself? What did he expect? What did he want? She was terrified of coming off as just another small-town girl. Surely, she thought, he came across them everywhere he went. Every assignment, wherever MERCENARY sent him, there was probably a girl similar to her. One intoxicated by his presence.

He turned around. His eyebrows lifted, and a grin grew. "What, I don't get a greeting? Did you forget my name?"

She shook her head and felt her face warm.

He waited a moment before rescuing them from the awkward silence. "This place is beautiful." His tawny eyes explored the glowing plant life that stretched over them. "What sort of plant is it? Or is it more than one?"

She took a step onto the pier. "The, uh, roots are in the mirror."

He dropped to a sitting position and swung his legs over the end of the pier. "Are you going to join me?" he asked. One of his arms motioned her forward as his gaze returned to the distance.

Her breath caught in her throat as she pulled the shoes from her grateful feet. She placed them next to his boots. The wood beneath her feet still held a bit of the day's heat, and the smooth boards felt therapeutic after her torturous walk. As she sat next to him, his scent, what she imagined Urba must smell like, pressed into her.

"I wasn't sure you'd come." His words were soft as if he was sharing a secret. "I'm glad you did."

She shakily exhaled false laughter and began swinging her feet. "I told you I would," she breathed.

He looked to her, and his warm stare drew her eyes toward his. "I spent most of my life in a small town like this one." He theatrically rolled his dark-amber eyes. "For years, all I could think about was getting out of there and moving to the big city. I wanted to see and meet new people every day, and I knew if I made it to Urba, I would."

"I know the feeling," she whispered.

"Yeah, I suspected we were kindred. But do you know what I learned, Gale?"

She shook her head.

"People are the same everywhere. There's maybe a dozen different archetypes, but I quickly found that few individuals are unique. Most of them just turn out to be different versions of the same sort."

"That's kind of sad." She studied his handsome face. He was older than her, but by how much she didn't know. As he spoke, his expressions briefly creased his skin in well-worn places, and this sign of maturity added to the urgency she felt to have him.

"No, it's not, Gale."

"What?" she breathed.

"It's not sad. Yeah, it was disappointing at first, but it ended up making me appreciate the few unique people with whom I come across." A hand reached over, and he caressed her neck. The movement, at first, was meant to draw her to his lips, but as his palm met its destination, he found his fingers wrapping themselves around a silver chain.

"You're so sweet," she gushed. Her heart sped at his touch. The desire to feel his weight on her multiplied.

He pulled at the silver chain and lifted what it held. His brow furrowed, and he attempted to resolve his confusion by squinting. "Is that essenia?" he asked.

She blinked a few times. It was as if he had gone off script. "Yes, uh, it's a family heirloom." She forced a smile and attempted to regain his stare with her own.

He moved the webbed setting and examined the black orb at multiple angles. "Fascinating," he muttered. "Is it black?"

She reached for it and freed the object of interest from its cage. "Yes, it's not only black, but…" She trailed off as she held the orb up. "It absorbs light. See how there's no glossy reflection?"

He stared at the essenia. It was as if her thumb and forefinger were around a hole in his vision. It didn't look three-dimensional. He ducked and craned his neck to see it at different angles. It was the strangest thing he had ever seen. "What mystics can you conjure with it?" he asked.

She shrugged and presented it to him. "For me it's ornamental, but my grandmother claimed it saved her life when she was a child. Her house was on fire, and she said that she was trapped in her room. As the flames ate their way toward her, she clutched it tightly and waited for death. But when the fire met her skin, she said she felt nothing."

He took the orb and looked at it more closely. It was warm and smooth. He stared into the dark crystal. There was something in it, but whatever it was evaded his sight. There was movement beyond the blackness, he was sure.

She watched as he examined the essenia. His attention was so fixed on the round crystal that she worried his interest in her had vanished. She hesitantly reached for the orb and closed a hand around it. His fixation broke, and he looked to her. Her warmth around him ignited a desire that was unlike anything he had ever felt. He craved her more than he had ever wanted anything.

She saw it in his eyes. The fiery lust that she had been feeling since she first noticed him was being reflected back at her. He leaned toward her, and their lips met. His body guided hers to the smooth wood, and she shuddered as his free hand traveled over her thighs and up her skirt.

She reached for the thick belt buckle over his waist; the tips of her fingers glided over the green essenia that rested there. She grabbed at the clunky obstacle and wished for it to break in her hands. His tongue danced before hers, and his scent dove into her. A greedy whine struggled from her, and he pulled away. While he removed his belt, she placed the black essenia back in its silver web.

As the weight of him pressed against her torso, air threatened to escape her lungs. The discomfort was brief, and when he found a proper position, she was glad she hadn't voiced her concern. Again, their lips met while he explored her.

As the pain subsided and pleasure filled its place, she found his gaze. The intensity of his stare was just as invasive as the rest of him, and she pursed her lips to please him. Sweat trickled from his brow, and the golden light of the setting gave him a glow that pushed her beyond anything she had ever felt. His name escaped her lips. "Oryn," she moaned.

Chapter 7

CIRRUS AWOKE ON Sagacious's lumpy sofa. Pain pounded his head with each beat of his heart. As he pulled himself up, the question of his location began to take precedence over the dull throbbing. A vague light shone around the edges of a nearby black curtain. He wobbled to his feet and pushed the fabric aside.

The truth of what he saw slowly registered in his fogged mind. He recognized the common layout of a drinking establishment. Two tetramach tables sat in the center of the room. The tavern's polished puce drinktop was so clean that the seto wood appeared coated in glass. A dozen short stools, with plush crimson cushions, rested beneath the uniquely feminine surface. The drinktop wove around the tavern in a seemingly unbroken stretch of smooth wood. Liquor bottles of various shapes and sizes lined the walls beyond the polished surface.

"Hello?" he croaked. He waited, but no one answered. For a moment, the possibility of partaking in what the unmanned tavern offered tugged at his mind. He turned in search of something to derail his growing desire. The distant sound of voices

42

crept to his ears, and he ambled back toward the couch. He stilled his breath and followed the faint noise to the spiral staircase. "Hello?" The rasped word absorbed more breath than expected, and it died as it left his mouth. No one responded.

He gripped the staircase's railing and started to descend to the lower level. His wrist and arm shook as he shifted his weight to the thin metal. The loosely supported staircase trembled with him, and he vainly struggled to correct himself. When he was halfway to the lower floor, the conversation sifted into coherence.

His dehydrated lips parted again, but before he could attempt to call attention to himself, the content of the conversation pieced together in his mind. At least one man and two women were discussing what sounded like a plan to bomb a reactor. When he reached the bottom of the stairs, he shuffled forward in an attempt to better understand the conversation.

The stiff fabric of his MERCENARY pants rustled as he stepped forward. He cringed at the discordant noise that sawed through the stillness. There was no doubt that the terrorists were seconds from discovering him. His right hand reached above and behind his left shoulder for the sword that wasn't there. His fist tightened, and despair filled him.

A buzzing noise fizzled in his ears, and he felt electricity pricking at his skin. His hair, formerly a greasy mess, was now a cluster of spikes. Warmth radiated from the essenia orb that rested within his heavy belt buckle, and he fought to rein in the erratic energy that was shooting from the cells of his body.

"Cirrus, you're awake already?" Sagacious asked. Her voice was apprehensive. She placed her bare thumbs into the miniscule front pockets of her short pants.

"Yeah, uh, where am I? What happened?" he asked. The growing charge within him vanished, and he felt his hair lose its stiffness.

"You passed out at the train station, remember? I didn't want to leave you there, and I don't know where you live, so we brought you back to Division Seven. I own the tavern, and I live down here." She shifted her weight and peered back into the kitchen. "How are you feeling?"

A few spikes of hair collapsed over his eyebrows, and he swiftly pushed them back up. Consciously, he reignited a base source of electricity, and his hair regained its rigidity. "I haven't eaten since..." he trailed off. He couldn't remember his last meal. "It has been hard to come by shill since MERCENARY cut me." It was his turn to shift uncomfortably. "I haven't been able to find another job yet," he mumbled.

"What'd you overhear, bro'?" Dash appeared at her side.

"I can handle this. Go back and have another drink with Julie."

Dash stood unmoving. His stony grimace fractured. "I told you this was a bad idea," he fumed. He glared into Cirrus's tired eyes. "You got a weapon on you?"

He spread his arms. "No, they took my sword back."

"A swordsman, huh? You were right, Sagacious."

"I'm always right," she responded. Her gaze shifted from Cirrus to Dash. "Go back to the kitchen," she ordered.

"Okay, okay." He took a step toward Cirrus and raised one of his arms. A tight fist formed. Muscles in the pale limb were forced into meaty lumps. "If you even breathe on her, I will crush your spine," he seethed. He turned and strutted back into the kitchen.

She rolled her eyes and looked back to Cirrus. "I'm sorry; he can be a little overprotective."

He bit his bottom lip and nodded. "I understand," he assured her.

"Let's go upstairs. We'll have more privacy up there," she explained.

"Sure," he sighed. He gestured for her to lead the way. He didn't want her to see how difficult climbing the stairs might be for him.

She began moving upward. "Do you want me to fix you something to eat?" she asked. "It sounds like you need a good meal."

He strived to keep up with her pace. "It's late, I couldn't ask—"

She cut him short. "You're not asking, I'm offering."

After reaching the upper floor, she strode over to the black curtain and slid it to one side. She led the way into the empty tavern and stepped behind the drinktop. From a short refrigerator, she pulled out a hunk of meat and placed it on a nearby wooden stand. Next, she opened a drawer and withdrew a large knife. She speared the meat and removed her hand before opening a nearby cupboard and pulling out a covered metal tray. After placing the tray next to the meat, she lifted the hemispherical top to reveal a misshapen loaf of bread.

"I overheard your conversation," he admitted.

"I had a feeling you did." She started slicing the bread.

"Why does your group want to bomb a reactor?" he asked. He couldn't think up a more tactful approach. His eyes were fixed on the meat in front of him.

She glanced up at him. "Oh, I suppose everyone in WAVE has their own reasons for wanting to bring Megacorp down, but our mission statement revolves around protecting Pearl. The vimstream is being exploited for profits, and we want to save the planet." She handed him the cream-colored porcelain plate that held the sandwich.

"Thanks," he sighed. He picked up what was making his mouth water. The savory meat was delicious. He closed his eyes and thanked Lazla for allowing this to happen. His concerns slipped away as he ate.

"Vim is the most precious thing on this planet. It's because of vim that we have essenia and the mystics that come with it. It's because of vim that we're here. When vim is gone, Pearl will be a lifeless ball of rock and water."

He swallowed another bite of his treasured sandwich. "I knew that you believed in stuff like that, but…" he trailed off. He stopped himself before he could question her sanity. He lifted the rest of the sandwich to his mouth. "Megacorp will charge you and your group with terrorism if they catch you. They'll roast anyone involved." He took a final giant bite.

She leaned against the drinktop and grinned as she noticed how much her old friend was enjoying her work. "Maybe," she admitted. "I see it this way: I don't want my daughter to grow up in a world in which everyone and everything are beholden to an all-powerful corporation. I don't want her only opportunity for a successful life to be serving Megacorp's war machine." She raised an eyebrow as she waited for a reaction. "They need to be stopped, and that begins by bringing down their main source of revenue," she finished.

He fought a mouthful of food as he attempted to speak. "And the planet?" A deformed smile broke across his dirty face.

"And the planet," she confirmed. "It's all connected. Megacorp, my daughter, you, me—it's all connected by the vimstream. It has to be protected, and no one on Pearl is stepping up."

He stared at his empty plate and sighed. "No one is stepping up, except for..." He couldn't think of a palatable term for her band of terrorists. "What did you call yourselves?"

"WAVE," she responded. "Our mission is to protect the planet and our shared heritage."

"It sounds..." he paused. It's some sort of cult, he thought. It's some sort of crazy enviro—

"We're not crazy," she asserted. "*I'm* not crazy. I know it sounds—"

"No, I know," he interrupted. "It's just that trying to blow up a reactor *is* crazy. Never mind the obvious fact that you'd be burned alive for just plotting to do it. The reactors are undoubtedly secured by first class MERCENARY soldiers. It doesn't matter if there are only two. They should be trained and prepared for anything."

She crossed her arms, and her mouth became a thin line. "Nobody in WAVE is under the impression that we're going to bring down an entire reactor. We're probably going to have to set off our bomb near it and hope the damage will be enough to impact the power grid."

His head bobbed, and he forced a smile. "Makes sense to me," he agreed. He met her questioning eyes and winked. "You have a daughter, huh? It's weird to think of you as a mom. Is big red the proud papa? I'm sure he's a nice guy when he's not threatening to crush spines."

She returned his smile and let out an exhale. "Dash isn't Darlene's father. He's an overprotective friend and an honorary uncle." She grabbed the plate and put it in a nearby sink. "He really is nothing to worry about."

"Oh? Because the homicidal glint in his eyes…" he began.

"Cirrus," she interrupted. Her gloved palms and bare fingers found a rag, and she started twisting it. "You're still the great guy that I remember, aren't you?"

He shrugged. "Who else would I be?"

"I was afraid that you might…" she trailed off and her gaze fell away.

"What? Turn you into MERCENARY? Fuck MERCENARY, and fuck Megacorp. They've ruined countless lives during their existence, even if their vim reactors don't harm the planet. You've been my friend since we were kids." Thoughts raced around his mind, and possibilities emerged. He tamped down the eagerness building in him while he steadied his voice. "If you need any help, I'm here for you." He scratched his hairy face and shifted his eyes from hers.

She stared at him. Part of her wasn't surprised that he was so willing to help her. He was dependable. He had always been dependable "Are you sure?" she asked.

"Of course." He grinned. "I have to pay you back for the sandwich."

She shook her head. "Cirrus, I have a little extra shill saved. I want you to have it."

"I'm not taking shill from you. I appreciate the offer, but I'm not going to—"

She held up a hand. "Wait," she interjected, "I have an idea. You can be a mercenary for WAVE! We'll hire you. You can use your skills and knowledge of the enemy to help us with our upcoming mission."

"I don't want to charge you—"

"Cirrus, you need shill, and you can help us. It's perfect. Don't pass up a financial opportunity."

"Is it that obvious that I need a job?" he asked.

"Yeah, I hate to break it to you, but when I found you at the train station—" she began.

"I found you," he interrupted.

She reached over and touched his nose with the tip of her finger. "Yes, you did."

Chapter 8

In the shower, Cirrus scrubbed the scum and dead skin from his body, washed his matted hair, and shaved the uneven beard from his face. When he stepped out of the steamy wash, he applied zeo-nut oil to the mess atop his head. He massaged the oil into his hair and shaped locks into spikes. Electric cracks filled the room, and water vapor vacated the space around him. As he stared in the mirror, he barely noticed the transparent bubble in which he stood. His essenia orb glowed from its place near the sink, and a green tint painted the room.

As his fingers slid through his hair and above his scalp, tiny sparks stung at him. The irritation barely registered in his mind. It had been some time since the volatile energy seeping from his body had caused him enough pain to be noticeable.

His reflection was a disappointing sight. His pastel blond hair was too long, and darkness surrounded his pale blue eyes. The sparkle in them was hard to discern in the dim green light, but the sporadic electricity still radiated from his pupils to the outer rims of his irises.

The unique qualities of his hair and eyes were a consequence of his vim trials. The features, although not physically debilitating, were a persistent reminder of his past. The Megacorp doctors and scientists, who had overseen his trials, informed him that these unusual traits would likely be permanent.

He volunteered to participate in the experiments after learning Aggeroth Wyvern had gone through similar trials. The essenia crystals varied in color, and the different colors allowed for different types of mystics. Aggeroth's abilities, however, appeared limitless to anyone who crossed his path. He conjured mystics from what appeared to be an internal rainbow of essenia. This combined with his conventional combat talents to make a virtually unstoppable soldier.

Others in MERCENARY were lucky to harness the power of their company-issued green essenia. Megacorp and their army preferred soldiers who could utilize the round crystals, but a natural ineptitude prevented most people from effectively drawing upon essenia. The ability to perform mystics was a divine art that called for an individual who could connect his vim to the crystals; a feat that required an innate understanding and comfort with both.

The Prime Project, which was believed to have bestowed Aggeroth with his unique abilities, was spearheaded by the world-renowned Garland Jecht. Prior to the Prime Project, as a Megacorp research scientist, Garland was responsible for discovering a practical means of converting vim into an energy that could be used to better the lives of everyone on the planet.

While this innovation in energy management should have allowed him the option of retiring early, he was under contract with the company when the discovery was made, and thus this very valuable piece of intellectual property was not legally considered his. Although he received no profits, Megacorp offered him a position at their university in Urba.

At the prestigious academy, Professor Jecht taught young men and women for many years. Eventually, his students' faces began to bleed together within his mind. This oddity was dismissed as a quirk of age by those with whom he came in contact and himself. But what started as an insignificant factor morphed into something much worse. The faces of nearly everyone in his life lost their perceivable characteristics, and he found himself lost in a world of blurred visages.

Not all individuals were clouded by the creeping cognitive disorder. The distinguishing features of one person proved to be exempt, and the professor consequently went to great lengths to keep this pupil in his life. Hewley Vayne was not an extraordinary student, and before Professor Jecht's life began to derail from its expected track, he paid the young man little heed. But as the encroaching mist blanketed his brain and fell over his eyes, he clung to the one person who somehow remained above the gray.

In hopes that it would slow or stop his problem, Professor Jecht sought out opportunities that would allow him to exercise his mental capacities. With his knowledge and experience involving vim, he solicited for and acquired funds from Megacorp. He expressed the intention of fulfilling the company's goal of producing MERCENARY soldiers who were self-sufficient in performing mystics. To assist in this endeavor, he secured the assistance of Hewley Vayne.

What occurred on the frigid island of Carlanda would never be known to anyone else at Megacorp. Less than a year after beginning the project, success was achieved. Their subject was transported by sea to Setra and then by land to the company's headquarters. By the time Aggeroth was received and roused from a state of suspended animation, Professor Jecht's resignation had been accepted, and his retirement in Highwind had begun. Dr. Vayne secured a position at a research center near the base of Mt. Terra where he was believed to be continuing his and his mentor's work.

A few months after moving into his estate, Professor Jecht was found dead, hanging in his foyer. In a brief note to his former student and assistant, he indicated that the shadow over his mind had finally engulfed the young man. Professor Jecht's property was left to Dr. Vayne, and the doctor assured Megacorp that his mentor's work would be continued.

Unfortunately, for Dr. Vayne and Megacorp, the secrets of the Prime Project's success died along with Professor Jecht. The young doctor found that both the professor's notes and his own memory were inadequate in directing him toward any success. To his knowledge, it wasn't as if he was missing requisite information.

While working on the Prime Project, Dr. Vayne was assigned to acquire, measure, and grade, vim samples. He was also tasked with the previously unheard-of feat of concocting a means of introducing foreign vim into a living being. These responsibilities proved to be very arduous for the young doctor, but when he believed he achieved success, his findings were purportedly adopted by Professor Jecht and integrated into a larger plan.

The professor documented his work well. There were half a dozen file cabinets in his mansion's cavernous basement along with detailed notes in a journal that he kept during their time on the northern island. All the available evidence pointed Dr. Vayne down a narrow path that should have, by his calculations, allowed him to find a way of not just replicating Professor Jecht's success, but implementing it on a large scale.

The acquisition of his own research center encouraged Dr. Vayne and his supporters within Megacorp. It seemed that the prospect of rolling out a standardization of MERCENARY soldiers, who were self-sufficient in mystics, was inevitable.

Dr. Vayne's much-publicized efforts, nevertheless, were a consistent failure. Cirrus's trials were overseen by the young doctor, and he was no exception. Some of Dr. Vayne's subjects became so deformed that they were euthanized. All soldiers were warned prior to the trials; however, many of them, including Cirrus, saw only the glory and success of Aggeroth Wyvern.

While no lasting harm was done to his body, the vim injections did temporarily impair Cirrus. Nausea, anemia, blurred vision, lethargy, hair loss, sensitivity to light, hearing loss, profuse nosebleeds, confusion, hallucinations, and personality alterations were the short-term side effects of his participation. As a result, MERCENARY discharged him.

After being dismissed, his sickly state was matched by mental anguish. Days and nights bled together as his understanding of time evaporated with his need to keep track of it. Depression weighed on him and suffocated his already weak ability to experience the emotional spectrum. As a result, life became easier, and the numbness was welcomed.

Cirrus rested his head atop a plush pillow. The smell of desert rose water wafted from it, and the spicy scent tugged at his nose. He turned to the soft sheet and nuzzled the cool fabric. The smooth material slid against his cleanly shaved face as he found comfort in the bed.

Gradually, he felt a slackening of the tension that had been pulling at his awareness since his expulsion from MERCENARY. He pressed his green essenia between both palms and rested his hands beneath his chin. A weak luminescence emitted from its core with each beat of his heart.

As the light of the round crystal radiated into his skin, his mind drifted into a soothing darkness. For hours, he lay in healing slumber. The heaviness of his melancholy slipped away, and he was pulled into the void.

The town of Highwind was alive with color and movement. Children ran and played as adults traded their goods in the town square. Cirrus looked to his family home. It sat intact only a few dozen meters away. Anxious to catch a glimpse of his mother and brother, he took a step toward the house.

A tremendous explosion ripped apart the harmony of the town. He strained to locate the noise. It appeared to have come from the Jecht mansion. Smoke billowed from behind the ancient ifia trees that blocked the massive residence from view.

Screams slashed through the air. He tried to run toward the cries, but he could no longer move. "Come on," he begged his paralyzed legs.

"It's too late," a familiar voice explained. "You cannot save the dead." His mother stepped to his side. Her curly, auburn hair swayed in the breeze. She was as beautiful as he remembered.

He avoided her icy eyes. "I'm sorry," he whispered.

"Look at me, Cirrus," she demanded. "I taught you manners, didn't I?"

He found her frigid glare. "I didn't know—" he began. Tears threatened him, and he blinked them away.

"Excuses, excuses, as usual," she muttered. "He's getting close; pay attention, Son." A knowing smirk crossed her face.

Aggeroth glided into sight. Exploring flames and dark billowing smoke accompanied him. His silver hair danced in the warming winds. His thin sword was in one hand, while his free hand orchestrated the destructive mystics that were burning the mountain town to the ground. He gestured at objects as well as onlookers, and quickly consuming white fire burst from his targets.

Cirrus's younger brother appeared through the dark smoke. His ivory skin was ghostly in the ashy air. The oversized silver buttons of his black leather jacket reflected white flames as the foolhardy youth ran toward Aggeroth.

The young man clumsily carried their father's sword in one hand, and the heavy weapon's tip bounced off the cobblestone street. Storm Stark skidded to a stop in front of his opponent in a futile attempt to block the man's path. His arms bobbed as he awkwardly raised the blade.

While growing up, Storm deviated greatly from his older brother. Shortly after Cirrus ran off to join MERCENARY, the younger sibling started courting his first love. She was pretty as well as intelligent, and the Starks welcomed the union. Storm and Jade married at an early age without objection from either family. No one could deny the devotion that the two shared.

He felt no ill will toward his brother or his brother's bride, but Cirrus neglected to attend their wedding. MERCENARY soldiers were expected to conform to strict codes of conduct, but he recognized that securing a leave of absence was not impossible. The truth was that he didn't want to face his family or his hometown.

There would be too many questions and comments. Returning to Highwind would've meant facing the consequences of his choices and explaining himself to people who would surely not understand. He preferred to ignore the fallout. They would've professed an acceptance, he knew, but an underlying disappointment and frustration would've been ever-present.

Although it proved to be awkward, Storm managed to get the sword upright. He proceeded to swing the blade at Aggeroth, who easily avoided the attack. The novice swung again, and again the master swordsman dodged the blade.

"Coward!" Storm hollered.

"He was so brave but so stupid," their mother commented.

Cirrus stared at her. "You don't mean that," he said.

She gestured to the scene. The man in black's bemused smirk was gone. With his sword pointed at his enemy, Cirrus's brother lunged forward. Again, his opponent stepped aside and evaded the attack. The hasty charge caused the young man to stumble and fall to his knees. Aggeroth swung his blade across

Storm's face. Blood rushed from the wound and coursed down his pale chin.

"No!" Cirrus yelled. He attempted to run to his brother's side, but his legs still refused to cooperate.

"Be quiet," his mother demanded. Her gaze was filled with disdain. "This is the best part," she said.

Aggeroth plunged his blade through the back of Storm's ornate leather jacket. The sword's initial force slowed as he pushed it deep into the young man. For a moment, the tip of the weapon poked out of the front of the jacket before a black boot stomped into the soft leather and metal was yanked from flesh and bones.

At the entrance to the brothers' childhood home, Jade and a new version of their mother appeared. The young wife screamed. Cirrus winced at the guttural noise. This second version of their mother reacted more appropriately than the one at his side. Her expression broke, and she wrapped her arms around the hysterical girl.

Aggeroth glanced in their direction. He dismissively waved his free hand, and the two women burst into white flames. The tight and controlled fire turned blue as it licked the wooden doorframe around them. Within seconds, the two figures were reduced to a smoldering lump of charred remains.

Cirrus looked to the woman at his side. His words trembled as he felt heat radiate from her false eyes. "I couldn't save them," he whispered.

"And do you know why?" her distorting voice asked. She brought her hands to her face and pushed her palms back behind her head. Aggeroth replaced his mother as he emerged from the facade. "You are not living up to your potential."

Cirrus strained to reach him. "You're dead!"

"Maybe, but I'm far from finished."

Chapter 9

EMMA LOOKED AROUND the train station. Young men and women were standing near and sitting on the orange chairs. Every few minutes, it seemed, a train was either screeching to a stop or chugging to a start. A mess of noise surrounded her. A few times, she began to pick up the thread of a conversation, only to lose it in the cacophony of sound.

She admired her white gloves and could see why they were so fashionable. With them, she felt the urge to make gestures whenever she spoke. It wasn't that she wanted to show them off, but their presence beckoned her to display them.

It was strange, she thought. Now that Oryn was on his way home, the only time she felt lonely was when she was in a crowd of people. Their expansive property kept her, for the most part, secluded. Often, she would find a string of days go by in which she didn't interact with anyone.

Her life wasn't completely isolated, however. She knew people at the market, and they always asked about Oryn. The owner's oldest son was eager to meet him. The boy was thinking about joining MERCENARY. She assured him that as soon as Oryn was back, she would introduce them.

She missed her daily visits from Irvin. The current delivery boy wasn't interested in visiting with her. Every day, his floating board zoomed up to her door, and he dropped off her letters without even a wave of acknowledgment. She didn't blame him. If their roles were reversed, she probably wouldn't have engaged her in conversation. Irvin was special, she knew, and she looked forward to his letters. He was still in Urba, at the university, but his class schedule precluded him from continuing his delivery route. He visited when he could, and she appreciated the rare occasions.

Irvin's letters became as much of a daily treat as Oryn's. She didn't admit it to him or herself that the drama of the young man's social life interested her, but it did. He went through relationships at a clipped pace; they lasted only a few weeks, despite his expressed desire to find love. He didn't ask for advice, but she offered it when she thought it was appropriate. He would settle down eventually, she knew. Young men just needed time to get their bodies and minds sorted out.

She interlocked her fingers, and they dug against the soft fabric. The desire to touch her face arose, but she stopped herself. The gloves were beautiful, but they picked up dust, dirt, and especially makeup far too easily.

The loud voice of a young woman arose out of the chattering that surrounded her. "Those gloves are gorgeous!"

She looked up. "Thank you," she replied. Her mood lifted, and it showed on her face.

"Where did you buy them? I've been looking for a pair made from snow squall, but they are impossible to find! I live down the street from a tailor, and he sells gloves, and I asked him if he had snow squall gloves, and he said yes and brought out a pair that was clearly not made from snow squall yarn." She raised her hands to show off her blue gloves. "I ended up going synthetic. I was hesitant, at first, but they are so much cheaper. I was able to afford four pairs with the shill that I had set aside for the snow squall pair. I was just fine with my decision, until I looked over and saw those."

"Well, thank you." Emma didn't know what to do with her hands. She clasped them and hoped that it looked natural. "Actually, I made them."

"You *made* them? You mean, like, you crubbed them? They must've taken ages." She bent slightly as she marveled at the object of her focus. "The yarn must've been tiny."

"It was," Emma breathed.

The young woman stood up straight and smiled at Emma. "Are you waiting for your husband too?"

"Yes, he should be home soon," she responded.

"Perhaps they were on the same assignment. Do you know where he was based? Lockheart, my husband, was based in the Mountain Region. I can't be more specific. He told me— several times—what town he was in, but, honestly, I never paid much attention." She briefly retracted her lips. "I'm sure you can relate."

"Oryn's assignment was in the Mountain Region as well. He was based in a small town with a vim vein not far from it. Highwind, I believe, is the town's name."

The young woman gasped and put one of her blue hands over her mouth while she started bobbing up onto her toes.

"That was it! That was the town! They must know each other. Maybe Oryn was Lockheart's captain. This was his first assignment."

"Oryn's not a captain." Emma frowned as she realized that he probably should've been promoted by now. He had made it to the fourth class, after years of hard work, but his letters never mentioned a promotion to captain.

"Oh, I'm sorry!" the young woman exclaimed "I just figured..." she trailed off. Her eyes fell to her blue gloves. "Most of the captains are, you know, more mature."

It took Emma a few seconds to figure out why the young woman looked so embarrassed. One of her white hands covered her neck. The makeup helped to conceal the crevices of time, but her damned neck must've given her away. She knew there were surgeons, atop the plate, who could do something about the sign of age, but she couldn't bring herself to visit one. Navigating her way up there, a place she had never been, was too daunting of a task.

"Incoming train from Peak Point, incoming train from Peak Point at Gate Seven." The announcement blared throughout the busy train station.

The embarrassment fled the young woman's face. "That's us, that's us!" She began bobbing again and reached toward Emma.

She hesitantly locked hands with the young woman as joy filled her face. "Yes, yes, it is! He's finally coming home." Her words fell from the sky and slammed into salt water as she started to sob.

The young woman stopped bobbing. "What's wrong?" she asked.

Emma shook her head. "I, I, I've just been waiting for so long," she explained. Her white hands went to her moistening face a fraction of a second before she remembered her gloves. She examined them. Makeup and the evidence of her tears were all over them. "Damn it," she whispered.

A screeching noise cut across the train station and was followed by a cheer that came from those who surrounded them. Every week the people who waited for this train were different, but they reacted the same way. Joy-filled smiles were plastered over the faces of the adults and their children. Some of them were dancing to music that only they could hear.

"Don't cry," the young woman implored. "He's almost here. Pretty soon, you'll look over—" Her speech broke off as she saw her husband enter the station. "Lockheart!" she screamed. Her eyes were now as glassy as Emma's. She glanced back to the older woman. "Everything will be fine," she said. With little regard for others around her, she pushed through the bodies toward her husband. He met her halfway, and the couple's lips found one another before a greeting could be uttered.

Emma watched as they merged. More tears rolled down her cheeks, and she resigned herself to the warm stream. She scanned the men in MERCENARY red who were filing into the train station. Each one, who was not Oryn, dragged at her spirit. Squeals of joy cut through the constant noise. She examined the men in red twice before the familiar despair filled her.

She collapsed into an orange chair and let the misery overwhelm her. Her head tilted back, and glowing strings were blurred by the tears that could no longer fall. Every week she went through this agony. Every week there was a young woman or a young man who would wait with her. Every week they would disappear into the crowd. And every week she was left alone to face the fact that the love of her life wasn't there.

She closed her eyes, and wetness trickled over her temples. Her strength was gone. The idea of making her way home seemed impossible. She wanted it to end. She wanted to fall into a void of nothingness.

It was at this point that her wish was partially granted. Emma slept. Despite the light in her face, the noise around her, and the hardness of the chair, her consciousness was buried in darkness. She didn't stir, and nothing interrupted the slumber for several hours.

"Wake up, Emma. We need your help."

The plea resurrected her, and she moved her neck into a more natural position. It ached. A hand went to massage it, and the dirty glove caused her to pause before she internally shrugged. It took her a few seconds to notice the little girl who was standing in front of her. The words, which had pulled her onto the shore of consciousness, fell into the inky sea.

"Uh, hello," Emma heard herself say. She slid up on the chair and sat properly for her audience. The child's white hair and emerald-green eyes were striking. Emma stared at the little girl and marveled at her unique beauty.

"My mommy needs help." Her voice trembled beneath weight.

Emma looked around the now nearly empty train station. Distracted, by the realization that the child was talking to her, an utterance fell from her lips as she tried to organize her thoughts. "Where is she?"

The little girl grabbed one of Emma's white hands. "She's lost."

She felt the small stranger pull, and she allowed herself to be guided across the train station. For nearly a minute, she permitted herself to be led. As they neared the exit, she stopped and found the child's gaze. "Where is your mommy?" she asked.

The little girl continued to lead Emma toward the exit. As the doors opened, the stink of the slums greeted them. Emma was about to question her again when their subject of mutual interest was found.

Her hair was as white as the child's. Later, in the years that would follow, Emma would tell herself and her adopted daughter that the woman's eyes were the same deep green as the little girl's, but in the following moments, as her life slipped away, Celeste's eyes barely opened. Emma crouched beside the wounded woman and looked for the source of the blood. Red wetness seeped from beneath her white dress as she cradled her midsection.

Emma's focus darted around the dark setting. "We need a medic," she breathed. "Maybe we can find someone who can use a curative mystic." The speed of her words increased as she noticed the amount of blood around them. "There were dozens of MERCENARY soldiers here not long ago. One of them will be able to use their essenia—"

Celeste grabbed one of Emma's hands. Her blood soaked through the gossamer yarn, and the older woman failed to notice the ruination of her hard work. "Emma Stillwater," she mumbled.

The panic in Emma vanished and was replaced by surprise. She reexamined the dying woman's face. Nothing about her was familiar.

"Oryn…" The word was barely audible, but its gravity pulled the attention of the older woman. "He wants you to move on."

"What?" Emma croaked. A wave of despair crashed into her, and she felt herself fall to a sitting position.

"Grace, do you remember what I taught you?" The fading voice was directed to the child.

"Yes," she answered. The little girl's reply shook and threatened to collapse into incoherence.

"Will you keep the treasure safe?" The airy question floated from the dying woman.

"Yes, I promise."

With what was left of her strength, Celeste squeezed the hand that she held. "Please, take care of Grace," she whispered.

Chapter 10

NOT LONG AFTER Sagacious fell asleep, Darlene jumped onto her bed and ripped her from her brief rest. Her first instinct was to order the child back to her room, but the girl's smiling face kept her anger at bay. She grabbed Darlene and began tickling her.

The challenge of being a single mother was amplified by the stress of WAVE's plans, and she was glad to have a man in her life who was so willing to help her. Often, when Dash decided to stop by in the mornings, he would bring her coffee. The gesture was an appreciated one, but she suspected that some of his visits were more to see Darlene than anything else. This didn't bother her. He occupied the child while she had a chance to read the latest news. His rapport with the little girl was unmatched.

Sagacious knew the reason for his feelings toward her daughter, and she allowed their bond to form and grow because of it. She couldn't imagine the pain that he felt. The constant sorrow in his eyes lessened when he played with the child, and she was glad that her and her daughter's love could be shared.

His visit was no surprise on that morning. Thoughts of his lack of confidence in her vanished when she saw what he was holding. A bag of Farron coffee beans was clutched in one of his pale hands. The exotic aroma accompanying his arrival was enough to bring a smile to her face.

The coffee traveled halfway around the globe before being brought into Sagacious's kitchen. The large island continent of Farron was home to the warmest of Pearl's climates. Its position on the planet both blessed and cursed the land mass with its sprawling jungles that spanned hundreds of kilometers. A few tribes dotted the outer rim of Farron, but for the most part it was wild territory.

With over four thousand kilometers separating it from the larger continents, any effort on Megacorp's part to tame its environment and colonize it would have been costly. The company dismissed Farron as a potential shill pit. A monopolization on the coffee supply would have been the only immediate financial benefit for claiming it. Although the massive island was rich in resources, it was Megacorp's accountants who decided to leave the tropical land alone.

The continent's scattered inhabitants showed little interest in the outside world. Their trade in coffee was a means of obtaining medical supplies and modern goods. The natives discouraged but tolerated tourism only from the wealthiest of individuals. Thus, while Farron coffee was available, it was hard to find and expensive.

"You're such a show off," Sagacious said. She gestured toward the small bag of roasted beans.

He dropped the bag onto the kitchen countertop. The un-mistakable aroma drifted across the room. "There's nothing else I'd rather spend my shill on," he replied.

She opened a cupboard and grabbed a dark wooden mortar and a short onyx pestle. "I know, I'd avoid paying Megacorp a single shill if I could." She rested the mortar and pestle next to the bag of beans. "Speaking of which, how long will our batteries hold their charge?"

After filling a pot with water, he set it on one side of the black plate that made up the stove's surface. He flicked a switch, and heat started radiating from beneath the pot. "Why do you ask?" he murmured.

"I checked the status gauge this morning, and it read forty percent." She tore open the bag and poured the beans into the shallow mortar.

"When's the last time you worked the generator?" he asked. He pulled the mortar toward himself. With his eyebrows raised, he met her gaze.

Her attention crept to the floor. She held up the pestle. "Three or four days ago," she admitted.

Dash snatched the stubby black stone and slammed it into the basin of the mortar. A few beans flew out of the small wooden bowl onto the off-white surface of the countertop. He began crushing the beans. "You need to do it every day," he muttered. The muscles in his right arm bulged against his thin short-sleeved shirt as he pulverized the coffee. "If you let the power cells drain, they'll lose their ability to fully charge. They should never go lower than eighty percent."

She retrieved the coffee press from the sink. "Don't overdo it. If it gets too powdery, it'll get caught in the plunger," she interjected.

He raised his hands and backed away. The onyx pestle dangled between a thumb and forefinger. "Damn it, Sagacious," he breathed. "Are you listening to me?" He flung the pestle onto the countertop. It clinked and rolled against the wall. "Do you have any idea how hard it was to build that thing?" he demanded.

She tipped the mortar over the coffee press's glass cylinder, and the crushed beans poured into it. "I know. I'm sorry, Dash." She briefly touched him, with one hand, as she grabbed the simmering pot with the other.

"Then what's the problem? You like riding your bike outside, right? It's the same thing. Except it's a trike, and when you pump the pedals on the generator, it powers your home and business."

She grabbed two mugs from a nearby shelf and placed them on the countertop. After pouring the coffee into both mugs, she picked up the steaming brews and handed one to him. "It just takes so long to build up the charge," she said. "I can't have the resistance too high, or it'll burn me out for the day. So, I set it on low, and then it takes me most of my morning."

He blew away the steam from his coffee. The childlike action softened his projected mood. "If you want me to do it for you, just ask."

"Dash—" she began.

"I mean, I figured the mighty Sagacious Gard would be able to handle…" He trailed off as he started sipping from the mug.

"It's not that I can't, but yes, I'd rather you do it," she admitted. A slurping noise sounded as she tasted the hot beverage. Its dirty, heavy body filled her senses. A hint of citrus slid across her tongue. "You're a strong guy, and you're a gentleman. You probably want to do it for me." She hid her smiling face behind her mug.

Chapter 11

CIRRUS SAT UPRIGHT. The essenia orb in his right hand radiated light into his palm. Someone or something had been watching him sleep. Eyes had crawled across him, he was sure of it. The sensation of another presence pressed into him.

"Sagacious?" he croaked. No answer came from the bedroom. Shadows around him were sliced in two by a band of illumination that shone from a slightly open door. Thoughts piled on top of one another as he grabbed his undershirt and slipped it over his head.

A thump sounded from beneath him. He flinched. The blond mess of hair atop his head snapped straight. The oil in it demonstrated its value, and the locks became spikes. He remembered the several candles, which lined the room, and raised his free hand. The essenia grew warmer as the candles flickered to life.

A high-pitched noise squeaked from beneath the bed. The image of scaly roglops flashed across his mind. The nasty pests were a plague in the slums. Their disgusting smell and mutated appearance earned them universal revilement. He shuddered at the thought of the winged insects.

He peered over one side of the bed and extended his free hand over the edge. Bluish-white strands of electricity formed between his fingers. His green crystal began pulsing with each beat of his heart, and the candles' flames elongated and grew brighter.

He was ready to discharge the energy that was building within him. It ricocheted from every cell in his body to the essenia and back again. His breath hastened, and his heart thudded.

A blurred shadow resolved itself off the edge of the bed. It was a small arm—the arm of a child. It stuck out from beneath him while its owner remained out of sight. Confusion assailed him. His charge died, and the bluish-white strands vanished. The candles' stretched flames dropped back to a more natural size.

"Hello?" he asked. He tried to remember the name of Sagacious's daughter. "Marlene?" he asked.

"*Darlene*," corrected the unmistakable voice of a little girl. "I'm Darlene—like darling," said the voice. "Who are you?"

"My name is Cirrus—like the cloud," he replied. Darlene's head popped out from beneath the bed. "What?" she asked.

Her resemblance to Sagacious was striking. Whenever the problems of adolescence became overwhelming, she had the habit of retreating beneath her bed. From the top floor of the Gard home, her room overlooked Cirrus's. Whenever her white curtains were draped across the window, he expected her to be under her bed. He would then make more of an effort to visit her on those days.

"I'm your mom's friend," he explained.

"This is where I play," Darlene stated. Her eyes danced as she examined the man above her. "Your hair is funny. Why is it like that?" She pulled herself into the dim light. She was wearing a simple pink dress. A skinny white ribbon was tied in a bow around her waist.

He sat upright and swung his thin legs over the bed's edge. "Yeah, it's a mess." A spike collapsed between his eyes as if on cue.

Darlene let out a joy-filled squeak and slapped her hands over her mouth. He stared at the rogue spike and pretended to be frustrated as he pushed it back up. Weak electrical pops sounded as his fingers ran through his oily hair. Faint flashes reflected off the girl's awestruck eyes.

"Wow!" she gasped. "You have mystics! You have mystics!" She jumped up and down. "More!" she begged.

He stared at the girl. Never before had he considered that his abilities could be used for entertainment. His training in the art of mystics had revolved around fighting. He had rarely practiced the skill since his expulsion from MERCENARY. How he might safely amuse her, he didn't know.

"Please!" she begged. She clasped her hands at her ribbon's bow and began to fiddle with it.

"Okay," he breathed. His feet lowered to the floor, and he stood next to the girl. She stared at him expectantly, and he returned her gaze with an expression of unease.

"Yay, Cloud!" A grin grew on her face.

"It's, uh, Cirrus—"

"Mystics!" she interrupted.

He raised his hands as she edged toward him. "Careful," he warned. "Mystics can be dangerous."

The essenia in his right hand grew brighter. His eyes followed the girl's as the soft green illumination filled the room. A soothing sound, like a thousand tiny bells, accompanied a sparkle that shimmered within the glow. A familiar feeling of warmth and exhilaration filled him. His heart beat faster, and his vision sharpened. After the light faded, a short-lived golden aura emanated from both of them.

Darlene clapped once and squealed like a sewer uribu. "Wow, wow, Cloud, wow!" she bubbled.

"Yeah—" he began.

"I gotta go," she interrupted. With smooth speed, she dipped down and reached beneath the bed. She leapt to her feet with a stuffed vaegah in hand. "Bye, Cloud!" she squeaked.

He was prepared to correct the girl again, but she ran out of the room. He tossed his green essenia on the twisted sheets and grabbed his jacket and pants from a nearby chair. For the first time, he realized how dirty the clothes had become. A layer of grime covered the thick and durable material. While the outside of the uniform was now blood red, the interior remained bright crimson. The pants were stiff and heavy as he pulled them over his scrawny legs. He cringed with regret as the rough fabric rubbed against his skin.

The gold-plated clasps of the jacket were chipped. Silver specks and scratches stood out against their surroundings. He sighed as he clasped them. A full-length mirror beckoned him from across the bedroom. He stared at his reflection. Memories flooded his mind, and he felt an urge to cast his gaze elsewhere. He pushed through his reluctance and glared at himself.

"I did it," he mumbled.

It was the first day of training. He stared at himself in a mirror that hung near his cot. His platoon's barracks buzzed with activity behind him, but his focus stayed on himself. He had never before felt such pride. He had never before felt so accomplished. A grin crossed his teenage face.

"Looking good, Stark." The tone was steady and confident. Xand Luneth's towering presence appeared beside him. His black hair flowed from his scalp and spilled over his crimson uniform.

While Xand claimed to be the same age as Cirrus, he made his counterpart feel thin and underdeveloped. With broad shoulders and the perpetual dark stubble of a man, Xand's mesomorphic body cultivated a masculine presence that was enhanced by his black mane. The physical dimorphism between the two caused a cognitive dissonance in Cirrus as he became fond of him.

He liked Xand's openness and confidence. The experience of becoming a MERCENARY soldier was both exhilarating and terrifying. It was a relief to share the process with someone whose self-assurance was infectious. But a bit of envy nagged at him, despite their ever-solidifying connection. And this caused him to feel an undercurrent of frustration that flowed beneath the surface of their interactions.

As they made their way to training camp, they shared a cabin aboard a silver train, which slipped between the mountains and across the grassy plains. It had been awkward, at first, sharing close quarters with a stranger, but the two quickly became friends. And as their time in training progressed, they became close.

"I heard we're picking our specialties today," Cirrus said. He refocused on his reflection.

"Yeah, are you sure you won't reconsider hand-to-hand? Then we'd have most of our training together." Xand pulled his hair behind his head. His impressive physique strained against his uniform as he tightened a red knot of cloth.

"Nah, I've always wanted to become a master swordsman." Cirrus ran his hands through his flat hair in an attempt to add a little dimension to it.

"That's right." Xand grinned. "You fantasize about being the next Aggeroth Wyvern." His dark eyes rolled.

"Who wouldn't?" Cirrus asked. "They say he's invincible."

Xand snorted. "No one is invincible, Stark. Everyone has a soft spot, and everyone can be defeated. It's just a matter of finding your opponent's weakness."

"Everyone has a soft spot except for you, right?" Cirrus smirked and caught Xand's attention in the mirror.

A serious expression settled on Xand's face. "The worst thing someone can do is not recognize his weakness."

Xand's words echoed in his mind. The candlelight within the bedroom grew dimmer as Cirrus's consciousness resurfaced from the memory. His eyes fell from the mirror, and he blinked away the tears.

He grabbed his belt and slipped it through the loops around his waist. He reached over and grabbed his essenia off the unmade bed. It flashed at his touch. He resisted a desire to hold onto it and placed the orb in his belt buckle. Before exiting the bedroom, he flicked a wrist, and the candles died.

Chapter 12

DASH PULLED THE cord of a lamp on his new desk, and the ball of strings beneath the shade dimmed. As soon as the light was completely out, he gave the cord another tug, and the office began to illuminate again. He looked around at the bare walls of the room. Squares of bright white highlighted the otherwise dirty paint. He stood and examined an edge of a square. A finger dragged over the border, and the greasy residue smeared at his touch. He grimaced. After a brief survey of the office, he reluctantly wiped the dirty digit against the waist of his pants.

Wispy clouds, beyond a nearby window, were sailing across the sky and above the Quartz Mountains. It was late afternoon, and Lazla's light was striking the gigantic crystals at an angle. As a result, a collage of rainbows painted the land before him. Within the colors, a herd of gauls were traveling. Their long legs moved in strides that shifted the weight of their bulky midsections, while the loose skin, which hung from their faces, swayed in the air. The young smaller gauls were galloping and jumping around the adults in a set pattern.

Arms reached from behind Dash, slid over his back, and wrapped around his skinny frame. "How'd you get in here?" he asked. "I've had enough of that damned secretary's incompetence. I don't care if she has a mouth to feed. She's out, done, fired!"

Fran squeezed her husband before releasing him. "You can't fire me. I know things, Mayor Black. Things that would have you pushed from your privileged perch of power. Your reign would be over before it could begin."

He wrestled with a smile. "Well, I guess I'm stuck with you."

"Stuck with me? As if anyone else on Pearl would work for a tyrant like you!" The faux passion that she evoked was amplified by her theatrical tone.

One of his hands reached for his wife's waist, and he coaxed her closer to him. Their noses touched, and he tilted his head to kiss her. She met his lips with hers, and he was again encircled by her embrace. The tips of her fingers ran over the bones and thin muscles of his back before wandering over his ribs.

The sound of a throat clearing interrupted the moment before it could advance any further. "Our newly minted mayor romancing a woman in his office before he's fully moved in? I don't recall that being a campaign promise."

Dash looked over Fran's shoulder and met Lucius's eyes. "I didn't make any campaign promises. I ran unopposed."

"Oh, I don't know about that. I heard the Leeks' varaluga came in a close second. The only reason I didn't vote for it was because of all the slobbering and spinning. Sure, varalugas are cute, but I could go without spittle at the town meetings."

David L Van Horne

Fran turned around and put her hands on her hips. "Hello, Lucius."

"Hello, Fran. Your breasts look especially buxom today. I can see why Mayor Black was molesting you." Lucius leaned against the doorframe as he drank in her reaction.

"You're as vulgar as that shirt is hideous."

Lucius looked down at the bright pink fabric that covered his chest. "This gorgeous shirt was custom-made for me and shipped from a very talented tailor in Urba. It is what's called high fashion. Only the most elite people on the plate can pull this look off, and I think I look amazing."

"Well, you're wrong. You look like you're wearing a costume."

"Dash, why is your wife so mean to me? I gave her a compliment on her swollen breasts, tantamount to congratulations by the way, and how does she respond? She insults my very expensive and very attractive shirt."

The amusement left Dash's face as he pieced together what Lucius meant. He craned his neck to look at Fran's breasts. They did seem slightly bigger. He remembered when she had been pregnant with Cindy, they looked the same. Blood drained from his face.

"Oh, apparently I pay more attention to your figure than your husband. I'm sorry, I thought it was common knowledge. You've clearly gone up a waist size or two. If I had wanted to be mean like you, I would have brought that up, but I guess someone in this tiny town should retain a modicum of class."

"Fran, are you—" Dash began.

"We'll talk about it after your meeting." She pulled from Dash and made her way around boxes of his things. Lucius waved at her as she passed by him; she responded with an annoyed shake of her head.

He sauntered into the room. "I don't envy you, my friend. Those hormones of hers are off the charts. You better hope this next one is a boy. Otherwise, in a few years, you'll need to be shipped off to that asylum in Medeal. You'll probably lose your hair too. It'll either fall out from stress, or you'll yank it out. And you don't want that. You wouldn't look good bald."

Dash briefly raised his spindly arms before he allowed them to drop to his sides. "Do you say whatever pops into your head? Is there no filter? By all holy light, Lucius, the last thing I need is knowing she's pissed and pregnant before our meeting with Megacorp."

Lucius clapped once and jumped. "I have a good feeling!" he squealed. "There are rumors in the mines. The manager of C mine told me that someone on his crew used to work in the Crystal Caves, and he said that Megacorp gave them new machines and tools and updated all their systems with new technology and software. All the owner had to give them was a fifteen percent share in the company! If I can get such a good deal, I'm going to bend over and kiss their rings."

"They contacted me on election day," Dash said. "My win hadn't even been made official. Some guy named Mr. Heidrig showed up at my door and said that the company was interested in making an acquisition. They must be interested in the mines."

"Well, if they want a complete sale, I hope they're ready to make me ridiculously rich," Lucius replied. "I want an estate in the heart of District One. I want the president of Pearl to be my neighbor. I love her. Now, there is a woman who can dress."

"She is kind of hot." Dash interjected. "You know, for an older woman."

"Hey, she has a thing for redheads, right? Maybe when I'm a billionaire, you can dump Fran and come be my assistant," Lucius suggested. "The president and I will be best friends, so I'll be able to put in a good word for you." He gasped. "You can have her, and I'll take Weiss! Hello, Daddy, am I right?"

Dash laughed and shook his head. "I don't know, man. I heard he's pretty intense. Did you hear how he killed someone during a meeting? A board member called for him to be replaced, and he just walked up to her and snapped her neck."

Lucius waved away Dash's words. "That's an unverified rumor. And even if it's true, whatever Daddy wants, Daddy gets."

Dash rolled his eyes. "Your taste in men is—"

Lucius brought his hands to his mouth as he noticed the time. "We need to get upstairs! The meeting is supposed to start in a few minutes!"

Dash looked to his office's clock. "Shi-it, you're right. Let's go!"

They rushed from the room and down the hall. Dash slapped the elevator's button and struggled to catch his breath. "How do I look?" he asked.

"Oh, don't worry about it." Lucius patted his shoulder. "I'm sure they've seen worse."

The two men stepped into the elevator, and Dash pushed the button for the third floor. "Hey, do you think, if you get all that new equipment, there will be less mining jobs? I mean, it would be great if you were able to get all that stuff, but will it, you know, put people out of work?"

Lucius shook his head. "No, well, there would be displacements, but I don't think there will be less jobs. There will be less of the jobs that exist now, but all the new additions will create replacement jobs. As long as people have desires, there will be jobs. The workers will have to retrain, but it shouldn't be too much trouble for them."

The elevator doors pulled apart, and they stepped off it together. Both men looked from side to side. Dash took a step to his left and paused, Lucius replicated the action.

"You don't know where the meeting room is, do you?" Lucius asked.

"It's my first day! I've never been up here, okay!" Dash hissed.

"Relax, look here's a directory." Lucius peered at the map. "It's down this way and to the right. Come on, Mayor Black. Try not to think about how fat and bitchy Fran is going to get over the next few months, and let's move!"

Dash's jaw dropped when he stepped into the meeting room. Three men in suits were seated at a table and facing the door. Behind them, two MERCENARY soldiers stood. On the hips of one of the men in red were two guns, while the other gripped spiked knuckles.

"Mayor Black, thank you for agreeing to meet with us so early in your tenure," Mr. Heidrig said. He stood and leaned over the table with an outstretched hand.

Dash quickly rubbed his sweaty palms against his sides as he strode into the room. He gripped the older man's outstretched hand and attempted to deliver an appropriate handshake. "I, uh, I'm happy to meet with you, uh, sirs."

Mr. Heidrig smiled and returned to his seat. "I see you brought a consultant. A very wise move, Mr. Black." His gaze touched on Lucius before returning to Dash.

They sat across from the Megacorp representatives. "Oh, this is Lucius Kyros. He owns the chail mines of Quartz Mountains," Dash replied. As he spoke, he nervously gestured to his friend.

Mr. Heidrig's attention flicked to Lucius, and he leaned back. The two men at his sides exchanged glances before they began whispering into his ears. After a few seconds, he nodded and again sat up straight. "I see, I presume, when the acquisition is made, you are expecting financial restitution for the mines?"

"Restitution?" Lucius asked.

"We are getting ahead of ourselves." Mr. Heidrig's attention returned to Dash. "If I may explain—"

"Sure, yeah, of course," Dash spurted.

The men at Mr. Heidrig's sides smirked at each other. "Megacorp would like to purchase this land. The mountains aren't of much interest to Megacorp, but the land surrounding them is property that we want to buy from the townspeople of Quartz Mountains."

"Wait, what?" Dash asked. "You want to buy our town?"

"No, Mr. Black. Megacorp wants the land on which the town currently exists. The company's instruments detected a vim vein beneath the town. We would like to build a reactor here."

Dash sat back as he tried to understand what he was hearing. "But people live here," he said.

One of the silent men appeared to stifle a laugh.

"Yes, Mr. Black, I realize that. What Megacorp is proposing is to buy the land from the townspeople. As we have done this many times, we are aware of the inconvenience for those involved, and so we are prepared to not only provide handsome compensation to every property owner, but also, we are offering to move the town up to ten kilometers away; wherever is decided. We will move every structure and install all the required utilities. In addition, we are offering free electricity for the people in your town, once the reactor starts functioning."

Dash looked to Lucius.

"The people of Quartz Mountains get their electricity from chail," Lucius interjected.

"Yes, Mr. Kyros, I understand that. If you own the mines beneath the mountains, we will, of course, compensate you. In addition, we will provide restitution for the loss of your business. Our standard offer in similar circumstances is an average of the past ten years' annual revenue."

"That's vaegah shit!" Lucius exclaimed. "My business is worth more than that."

"It may currently be worth more than that, Mr. Kyros, but you must realize the loss of demand once our reactor is in place."

Dash cleared his throat as a thought emerged. "Most of the townspeople work in the chail mines."

"Yes, Mr. Black, I understand that. I cannot promise a position for every applicant, but the reactor will need personnel. I would encourage all qualified individuals to join our team."

"What if some of the townspeople don't want to sell their property?" Dash asked.

"That's not uncommon, Mr. Black, but given that a majority of the town's property is public, if you agree to our terms, we can and will begin construction. Usually, that convinces anyone who previously refused to sell. If it comes up, when you speak with your constituents, please explain to them that if they wait to sell, the amount that we will offer will be lower."

Lucius shifted in his seat. "Those reactors poison the land around them. I've been to Urba. I've seen the slums. You can't find a blade of grass for dozens of kilometers around the city."

"Mr. Kyros, Urba is a very unique location. There are eight reactors there. We are proposing to build one here."

"Just a little bit of plague, that's all, right?" Lucius spat. "You can't just move the town. The Quartz Mountains are a part of the town. For fucks sake, it's what we call the damn town!"

"With all due respect, Mr. Kyros, I would like input from the mayor."

Dash exhaled and shook his head. "Lucius is right. The town can't be moved. We love this land. We are this land. We are the Quartz Mountains. And I've seen images of the slums. I've seen what vim reactors do to the environment."

"But, Mr. Black, surely you will want to discuss this with your constituents before you decline this very generous offer."

Mr. Heidrig motioned to one of his associates with a finger. The silent man quickly opened a folder and slid a sheet of paper toward Dash.

Dash's stare didn't break from Mr. Heidrig. "No, I'm sorry. I know my town. No one will go for this, no matter how much shill you offer us."

The silent men again exchanged glances. Mr. Heidrig sighed and stood. "Very well, Mr. Black. We will find another way to proceed."

Chapter 13

A HANGOVER PRESSED into Cirrus's head and spun through his gut. He endeavored to ignore the tavern above Sagacious's apartment. The question of whether she would take issue with him asking for a drink ran through his mind every few minutes, and he narrowly avoided the awkward scenario.

When the illuminated mesh of the apartment started to dim and flicker, the already moody Dash stomped off through a nearby doorway without explanation. Cirrus breathed a sigh of relief as the contentious chemistry between the three was disrupted. The heavy door slammed shut behind Dash.

"What's his problem?" Cirrus asked.

Sagacious sighed and continued cleaning up after their meal. "It's the generator. Dash is worried about his baby."

The tangled strings above them flickered and dimmed before going dark. A bang came from behind the door. "Shi-it!" Dash roared.

One of Sagacious's arms bumped into a mug. A shattering noise filled the kitchen. "Shit," she echoed. A few seconds passed before Cirrus heard a scraping sound from her direction. A flame sparked to life in her hand. She grabbed a half-melted stump of wax from over the sink and brought the fire to the candle's wick.

"Do you have a broom?" Cirrus asked. His attention flitted around the dark room.

"Don't worry about it; I'll take care of it." She stepped over the shards.

A clanging noise sounded from beyond a nearby wall. "*Son of a whore!*" Dash bellowed.

"Will you give him a hand?" she asked. The candle's flame wavered as she returned the stump of wax to its place above the sink. She pulled a broom from somewhere in the darkness and began sweeping up the broken mug.

Cirrus stared at her. He didn't want to spend any more time than necessary with Dash. "He won't want my help," he responded.

She let out a forced laugh. "I'm sure he won't, but will you ask him anyway, please?"

"Okay," he sighed.

The room that contained the generator was lit by a lantern on the floor. It shone its light on what appeared to be a tricycle that was fixed in place by four metal bars. Several colored wires ran from the restrained vehicle's bulky midsection and wrapped around the thick bars. They were connected to four towers, which were melded together. Buttons and dark screens showed on the faces of each tower that made up what Cirrus assumed to be the generator.

"Damn you, you little sin shit," Dash grunted. His voice came from behind the generator before he stumbled into sight. "Fucking roglops!" he yelled. A hiss rose and fizzled in response.

"They're drawn by heat and feed on electricity," Cirrus explained.

Dash flung a tool at the unseen pest. As metal clanged to the floor, a droning buzz arose and headed straight for the red-haired man. He ducked to evade the flying pest. Its large transparent wings were invisible in the soft light. It dove toward him and swooped above his head. He blindly swatted at it. The unmistakable stench of roglops filled the room, and Cirrus's stomach quivered.

The large bug dove at Dash again, and he sank deeper into a crouching position. "Go get Sagacious, she has a net," he ordered.

"I can take care of it," Cirrus assured him.

Dash glared at him. "Their shells are rock hard, you can't just—" He hopped to one side to avoid the vicious creature's pursuit.

Cirrus extended his fingers at his sides and waved them independently of one another. The roglop's attention shifted from Dash as a charge built within the ex-MERCENARY soldier. The creature's whining chatter changed from angry to curious. The monstrous bug sensed that the atmosphere was changing as unseen fuzz filled the room.

Cirrus raised his arms, and a wavering bolt of bluish-white electricity formed between his hands. The roglop left Dash's personal space and zoomed toward the energy. Its six legs twitched while its hornlike pincers pulled apart. When it was halfway between the two men, the bolt vanished.

Cirrus turned his palms to the confused creature, which burst into orange and yellow flames. The fire consumed its wings in a flash, and it dropped to the floor with a clunk. Flames chased the panicked creature as it ran in circles and whined in pain. Finally, there was a muffled popping, and the roglop lay still. The disgusting stink of the dead insect was masked by the smell of its charred remains.

"Whoa, that was awesome," Dash said. He stood up, but his eyes stayed fixed on the roglop's remnants. His words were no longer dripping with contempt.

"Uh, thanks," Cirrus replied. "Do you need any more help?" He hoped the answer was no. Even with Dash's changed inflection, being alone with the explosive man made him uncomfortable.

Dash rubbed a hand over the stubble atop his head and peered behind the towers. "It chewed through a few wires. I think I can fix them. The real problem is that it drained what was left of the power. It's going to take a while on the trike to fully recharge the batteries..." He trailed off. "Hey," he spurted, "I think there might be a way you can help."

Cirrus waited for an explanation. After an awkward silence, he asked, "How?"

A few hours later, the illuminated mesh that lined the ceilings of Sagacious's apartment and Seventh Heaven were shining brightly. The members of WAVE assembled around one of the tables in the tavern. The first patrons wouldn't arrive until the late afternoon, and the group was free to discuss their plans without fear of being overheard. The air in the room was stagnant and dry. No small talk was attempted. Trepidation hung like the glowing tangle of strings above their heads.

Brack dwarfed Cirrus when they were introduced. Sagacious could tell by her old friend's grimace that the bear of a man's handshake was brutal. Few words were exchanged, and they failed to make eye contact.

Wells, a much shorter and thinner man, seemed at first to not be as perturbed by the ex-MERCENARY soldier in WAVE's midst. However, any rapport that might have existed between the two evaporated when Cirrus pointed out that the gun strapped to Wells's waist would likely be useless against any MERCENARY soldiers guarding the vim reactor.

Julie was the only member of the group, other than Sagacious, who didn't seem put off by Cirrus's presence. Rather, her reaction was out of character to her typical emotional range. The normally cheerful and chatty young woman was virtually silent in his presence. She stumbled over her words and seemed unable to meet his gaze with her own.

Before the two women joined the others, a zealous grin flashed across Julie's face. Sagacious attempted to return the signal with equal enthusiasm but found it difficult. Although she would be forever fond of Cirrus, she recognized a deep sorrow within him. The last thing Julie needed, Sagacious thought, was to fall for someone so broken.

Cirrus's eyes shifted from Sagacious to the others as WAVE briefed him on their plans. The raid was scheduled to take place early the next day. He sat silently and listened while the group of terrorists laid out their scheme.

"Do you think you can get us in?" Sagacious asked.

"Honestly..." Cirrus rubbed his eyes and paused.

"What?" The annoyance in Dash's voice was apparent even to him.

Cirrus shrugged. "It sounds like you're not very prepared."

"We have a bomb, and we have a plan for escape. Yeah, things could be better. That's why you're here," Dash seethed. He continued to avert his glare. It was how he attempted to show some civility toward the ex-MERCENARY soldier after witnessing his competence in the art of mystics. It wasn't much, but it was the most that anyone could expect from the short-tempered man.

"What will you do if I can't get WAVE inside the reactor? You're planning on setting the bomb off outside it? What then? There are surveillance lenses around every reactor. There might be only two soldiers on patrol, but their eyes will be everywhere. The second we get near the reactor they'll know.

"They must've seen you when you were on recon, and you're lucky that they left you alone. They probably assumed you were harmless. But I can promise you that a group of six approaching the reactor, before Lazla's first light, will get their attention. And even if we somehow stay undetected, bombing the reactor from the outside is pointless."

"We want to make a statement," Sagacious asserted. Her arms crossed as she stared at him.

"I know, and that's great. But I know Megacorp too, and they'll spin something minor like that into nothing. They'll claim it was a technical problem. No one outside the company will know who did it, or why." Cirrus's eyes sparkled as they darted from Sagacious to Dash and back again.

"If we can get under the site's umbrella, we'll be able to arrest their hub," Wells interjected. "We'll block ingoing and outgoing communications and broadcast from our location. We should be able to subvert every Megacorp stream." A casual confidence gave his words a flippancy that was foreign to the tone of the room.

"So, you think we'll have enough time to broadcast a message *and* set off a bomb?" Cirrus asked.

Sagacious fought to keep from sounding annoyed. "Do you think you can get us in or not?" she asked.

Cirrus sighed. "I can try. When I left MERCENARY, I kept some things that might help us out. They're in a locker at the Division Six slum-level train station. I'll grab what we can use."

It came as no surprise to Cirrus that Brack, Wells, and Julie were just as unprepared and ignorant of the situation as Sagacious and Dash. WAVE and their plan seemed to be little more than a handful of extremists who were bent on taking down Megacorp. Their collective blind spot was so large that it eclipsed the obvious conclusion: they would surely die. Cirrus listened and nodded as assumption after assumption was made. Several times he stopped himself from shattering their expectations.

Yet despite their near-zero chance of success, he decided to go along with them. He could see no better option for himself. And while WAVE's plan was foolish, it held a couple of possibilities. If they failed, he would be dead. Part of him yearned for the peace that death would bring. He didn't have the courage to kill himself, but if he died in battle against Megacorp, he would welcome the end.

The second possibility was far less likely, but he entertained it as their meeting stretched on. Perhaps MERCENARY would take him back if he thwarted this effort. He believed it would surely fail with or without him. By this time the next day, he supposed, the members of WAVE would be burned carcasses. Darlene would probably be shipped to an orphanage some-where in upper Urba—a fate likely better than growing up be-neath a tavern in the slums of Division Seven.

If they were going to fail, why not use this opportunity to return himself to MERCENARY's favor? Although he thought his treatment by those in charge had been horrible, being a sol-dier had nonetheless given him a purpose. He had forged his own life. He had made friends. He had found love. If he could get back in the ranks, he believed, he could become happy again.

"Let's go over our best-case scenario." Sagacious's words broke through Cirrus's thoughts. She rolled out a map on the table. "Once the bomb goes off, Megacorp will be after us. They'll search for digital evidence of us. It should make it dif-ficult, hopefully impossible, for them to track us if we travel to and from our meetup location separately and at separate times. Duck into restaurants and leave through bathroom windows. Go in circles. Be creative.

"We will meet up here." She pointed to a red dot near the edge of the plate. "It's a café near the site's front entrance. From there, we will split into three teams. Dash and I will handle any MERCENARY soldiers who show up." She glanced from

Wells to Brack. "Are you sure, once we're under the reactor's umbrella, you'll be able to arrest the site's hub?"

"Yeah, it'll be encrypted," Brack said. "But I can crack it. Once we're under the site's umbrella, I have a device that will block their connection to the network. The hard part will be getting my computer access to the network. It's not a big problem though, it will just take a few minutes of hacking after we're in place. I'll cloak our signal to conform to—"

Sagacious held up a hand. "I trust you." She looked to Julie and Cirrus. "You two will find the reactor's core and set the bomb's timer for thirty minutes. Cirrus, you'll guard Julie and lead her through the interior of the building.

"While you two are making your way to the core, setting up the bomb, and heading back to the entrance, we'll be broadcasting WAVE's message on every channel and station owned by Megacorp."

"Then we haul ass," Wells said.

"We will need to get far fast," Julie chimed in. "If we manage to set off my bomb in the reactor's core, there will be a chain reaction and the whole place will blow."

"Keep in mind, as soon as you do your broadcast, they'll be hunting for us," Cirrus said.

Silence filled the room as they pondered the plan. Success would mean the total demolition of one of Urba's eight vim reactors. Failure, they knew, would mean their end. Cirrus started weighing his options again. Sagacious considered Darlene's future. Dash anticipated his revenge. And the others found themselves lost in thought.

Chapter 14

THE PATH THAT Cirrus chose, from Division Seven to Division Six, was not an extended one, but it went through one of the slums' several garbage dumps. Here on the border between the two divisions, heaps of debris were piled so high that less than a hundred meters of free space existed between the trash and the bottom of the plate.

A slew of sickening odors assaulted Cirrus's nose. They mingled together to create a rancid stew that was both biological and chemical. His gag reflex kicked in, and the prospect of finding another route became an urgent desire. After a few minutes, however, he became desensitized to the sickening fumes and forced himself through the disgusting landscape.

He became lost within minutes. His sight was limited by the mountains of trash, and there wasn't a logical path or sign to point the way. With no one to ask for help, he picked a direction and tried to keep to it.

The sword on his back was a gift from Sagacious. She said it was a family heirloom, and he felt awkward accepting it. The blade of the sword was wide, and the weapon was heavy. It pulled on him, and the straps of the battle belt dug into his shoulders.

Earlier, after the others had gone their separate ways, he sharpened the dull blade and practiced with his new weapon. He found its weight cumbersome, but it gifted him with momentum, which was useful when performing unconventional movements. It felt accustomed to his hands, and he liked it.

Eventually, the mounds of filth began to grow farther apart. At the edge of the junkyard, a short fence staggered in an outline around the piles of trash. A playground's rusted equipment matched the browning tangle of metal that separated Cirrus from the long-abandoned park. There was no visible gate, but none was necessary. He pressed his palms together and concentrated on the barrier. Moving the earthen elements was difficult, and to manipulate metal required a narrow temperature fluctuation, which was a consequence of controlling the air. Therefore, to change and move metal called for a competence in the task of using mystics from two elements at once.

The fence was no serious obstacle. He knew he could have climbed it, and if the soles of his boots would have proved too wide for the spaces between the links, the aged iron was so rusted that he figured he probably could have broken through with a few strategically directed kicks. But this was an opportunity to practice honing his skills, and he took it.

The fence began rattling. Bits of brown debris flew into the air, and the smell of oxidation replaced the area's rancid stench. Glowing spots of redness spread on the metal, and the links stretched and warped as Cirrus pulled his palms apart. Gravity dragged at the distorting fence, and the weakening metal threat-ened to fold. Recognizing this, he attempted to keep it standing as he created an opening. But the tasks of simultaneously ma-nipulating both the earthen and air-based elements proved to be too much, and he allowed it to collapse.

As he walked by the old and decaying equipment, he thought of the children who must have played there. Ghosts of joy flashed before his internal eye while laughter sounded from just beyond his perception. The crunching of his heavy boots against the gravel resonated across the dreary area, and the emptiness yawned around him.

Leaving behind the desolate playground, he made his way to the center of Division Six's slums. Several one-story build-ings stood across a brick street. Neon signs hung above win-dows announcing the presence of light and life. Some of the people, who came into view, were sitting on the stoops of build-ings or on the curbs of the street. Their vagrancy was made clear by their respective jars and upside-down hats. Already the lifestyle seemed foreign to him.

"Look lady, I don't want to hurt you. Reach into the pockets of that pretty dress and hand over your shill." The gruff voice came from Cirrus's far right. An unkempt beard grew from the dirty face of the man. His stained clothing hung loosely over his lanky body, and the dark semicircles beneath his eyes seemed to draw in the slum's dim light. In one hand he held out a silver revolver.

She was much shorter than her attacker and appeared too delicate for the slums. Her white hair was pulled back behind her and held in place by an iridescent clasp. Her subtle beauty was complemented by a bouquet of pink flowers in her hands. A petal glided into the gray after it peeled from its shuddering source.

"I told you, I don't have any." She shoved the flowers at the man. "Here, take these, they're all I have."

"I don't want your flowers!" the man shouted. "Give me your shill, or I'll put a bullet in you!"

"Hey!" Cirrus yelled. He jaunted over to the two. His heavy sword smacked his back with each footfall. "Didn't you hear her? Back off, she's dry." He readied himself to draw his sword; a charge coursed through him.

The gangly man's sunken eyes shifted to Cirrus. The hand holding the revolver dropped to his side, and his thick salt and pepper eyebrows rose with surprise. "M-M-MERCENARY? I'm sorry, sir. I didn't—"

"You need to make your own shill," Cirrus interrupted. He gripped the handle of his sword. "Apologize to the lady, and be on your way."

"S-S-Sorry miss," he sputtered. His birdlike legs moved in lengthy strides as he hurried away.

Cirrus watched the man until he disappeared down an alley. "Are you hurt?" he asked.

She peered up at him. Her emerald eyes were piercing and somehow familiar. "Thank you," she breathed. "I'm fine." Fear lingered in her tone. She focused on his hair before directing her gaze to meet his. The warmth of her stare scared his eyes downward to the almost foreign sight of color and life.

At this moment, the needle of progression paused. A trickle of whiteness slipped from a milky-colored orb that was hidden within the soft nest of the young woman's hair. The ghostly dribble passed into her flesh where it burst into countless ethereal particles. Each piece of the foreign presence fell into its assigned cell, and adjustments were made to the host organism. When every aspect of the young woman was inhabited and ready for operation, her stunning green eyes lost their color, and her consciousness was temporarily shelved in its proper place.

"How many times must we go through this, Maladaa?" The voice that came from her pink lips was dusty with age. The syllables stretched as they broadcast from beyond all that could be known. Her white eyes glared at the downturned face of the man before her.

Cirrus remained stationary. His eyes were fixed on the flowers. All was still as Baladaa sought to confront her adversary between the moments.

"Please do not insult my intelligence, old friend. I know you are here. I know you are camped within him. What I do not know are your intentions. Why are you here again?"

Cirrus's frozen expression cracked as the corners of his mouth became a grin. "You don't think I'd really tell you, do you?" Black eyes looked up from the flowers. "But you're surprised though, right? That I came back here, I mean." Maladaa strolled around his timeless nemesis. The insect-like eyes bore holes in the young woman. He wondered if the light half, the white half, the positive to his negative, the up to his down was really as clueless and tired as she seemed.

Baladaa was sure to keep her rival in front of the borrowed body. She felt danger soaring toward her, and she would not allow Maladaa to seize the opportunity that he was manufacturing. "I will admit that your antilife was effective, but they stopped it. We came to a draw. This place is a dead end. Let them be and meet me on a more appropriate field of battle," she said.

Maladaa chuckled, grabbed the white-haired woman's wrists, and pulled her close to him. Her flowers fell to the ground. "Oh, let's not be so cold, *old friend.*" He stepped toward her, and she was forced to step back. Their surroundings smeared. The dreary setting of the slums was replaced with a field of wild flowers and snow-capped mountains. The clean air carried with it a sweet scent that washed away the nasty stink of the previous time and place.

The blond spikes atop Cirrus's head pointed to the sky as Maladaa released her and took a few steps from the pebble-covered path. "Pearl has to be one of my favorite planets." His dark stare found Lazla. "The blue star is a nice touch, but you and I know a yellow one would last longer."

He bent down and examined a jagged purple flower. "I suppose there are probably trade-offs that I haven't considered." Maladaa grabbed the stem of the flower and snapped it free of the ground. He brought it closer to his dark eyes. At the center of the swirled spears of purple was an orange powder that appeared to be releasing a bit of shimmering mist. "You really out did yourself. At least there's a legitimate reason for your insufferable pride."

Baladaa's gaze narrowed on where Maladaa had picked the flower. It regenerated in an instant. "Our pride is equal and shared."

"I can't tell you how frustrated I was by your recent stunt," he interjected. The flower in his hands fell apart and became dust. He stared at her. Heat radiated from Cirrus's chest, bounced off the thick uniform, and fueled the rage that was building within the body. Under his arms, sparks snapped at his skin while electricity crawled over his scalp. Maladaa treasured emotions. They were a dangerous and unpredictable element, and this fact was one of the reasons he was back on this speck in space.

He yanked back the sudden urge to ram Cirrus's heavy blade into the young woman. "I was under the impression that there was an unspoken agreement. I thought you didn't want the fabric to unravel again, and I don't want to deal with the complexity that would come with—"

"I may never defeat you, Maladaa." It was her turn to speak. "I have grown to accept that. Perhaps it is for the best. But you must know that I will do whatever is necessary to prevent you from defeating me. If that means unraveling the fabric and starting over, so be it."

The laughter that burst from the face of Cirrus Stark briefly surprised the foreign presence within his body. Maladaa composed himself and neared her again. "I don't believe you. I sense your attachment; you love your pets! And I know you're pleased with yourself." He spread his arms and his gaze touched upon their surroundings. "If I can appreciate the beauty of this life bearing world and the trillions of others, surely what you feel for all creation is great."

"Why are you here?" she demanded. "There is nothing left for you on Pearl. Your antilife was neutralized, and we both know I will not allow another to make its way here. Let them be. Let them live and die. It is a fair balance. Let us move onto another plane where we will each have a chance at victory."

He tilted Cirrus's head up, closed his eyes, and inhaled. "Maybe I'm on vacation. Did you consider that?" His eyes peeked open. The cloudless sky poured into him. The damaged man's perspective never ceased to be intoxicating.

"I was under the impression that you abhorred my beauties. Black holes draw your appreciation. You do not enjoy starlight; you cannot appreciate the artistry of creation. Something is happening. You are doing something. There is something that is different." Baladaa paused as she examined all available factors. "What is it? What are you doing? I am missing something. There is something that I cannot see."

Any flippancy that had emerged vanished as he felt Baladaa grasping into all the corners and crevices of Pearl. He was confident that she'd come up with nothing, but the words that breathed from the young woman's mouth were enough to cause him to question his surety. "How about we make a deal to put your worries to rest?" he asked.

"What do you have in mind?"

"I'll abandon Pearl forever and follow you to whatever plane or planet you want, but you have to promise that you will also never return. No more playing with your precious vim. No more marveling at mystics. I'll let the creatures of this place play out their act without reaching in and spoiling the fun if you promise to be as restrained."

"How can you think so little of my intelligence after all that we have been through?" she asked. "You have done something. I cannot see it, but I sense it. The ground is shifting, and that is why you are wishing me gone. That is why you don't want the fabric to unravel."

Frustration bubbled up within him. She was going to do it again. She was going to thwart him. This dance would go on forever. Neither one would gain the upper hand. The perpetual impotence of being one side of divinity was a curse that would never lift. He rubbed Cirrus's palms over his eyes and sighed. "I hate you so much," he mumbled.

"You hate me?"

Cirrus's arms fell to his sides and their eyes met. "Yes, I *hate* you."

"You are not capable of hating—"

The sword was in Cirrus's hands before Maladaa could stop himself. The irritating sparks that were torturing his temporary body fueled an explosion of fury, and he raced toward her. In that flash, he didn't care if his actions would cause the fabric to unravel. He would deal with it. They would start over again. From the first hydrogen atoms to the uranium that would lie within the thrice backwashed cosmic debris. It would happen again and again. He would push one side while she pushed the other, and they would be stuck in this maddening dance forever.

Chapter 15

HIS ACTIONS WERE slowed by the weight of the sword, and this gave her time to slip out of the way. When Cirrus's back was to her, she gripped his shoulders and stepped toward him. The sky darkened, and the land flattened. The white pebbles beneath their feet became ruddy dust. The air was dry, and burnt wood tainted it with a smoky scent. A spent bonfire lay not far from them. Around the glowing embers, six figures slept in their frozen moment.

"What is wrong with you, Maladaa?" Her voice carried with it an equal amount of concern and anger. "How can such a simple guise cause such an influence? You are not rash. You are not emotional. What is going on? I demand an answer."

More laughter erupted from Cirrus's mouth. "She wants to know what's going on!" he shouted. "She wants to stop me. She wants me gone. She wants to be the sole power. Can you blame her? I don't blame her. After all, I want the same thing."

Baladaa edged herself between the six sleeping figures and her rival. Next to one of them, the glow of the embers glinted off a metal staff. She swooped down and grabbed it. Continuing the unbroken movement, she held the staff horizontal in front of her. "You are going mad in that body. You have clearly been in him for too long. Leave him at once and gather yourself in the ether."

Maladaa pointed Cirrus's sword at the sleeping figures. "I don't want to kill anyone. I don't want to unravel the fabric. Do you think I like governing electrons and other bits and particles for ages? I don't. The needle rarely advances so far. Neither you nor I want to throw it all away, old friend!"

As he paused, he returned the sword to its place on his back. "Let's leave this place together. Let's go and slug it out on that thread near the knot. Surely one of us will find something there." He stuck out a hand. "Come on, Baladaa. If I'm not here to make mischief, if you continue to block my efforts to escort a new antilife to this planet, how could I do anything that might tip the balance in my favor? My vacation is over. Make this deal, and save your precious pets. If you don't..." He raised Cirrus's other hand, and flames appeared above it. "I'll do it. I won't hesitate. I'll kill her or both of them, or the whole lot right now. And it will all fall apart, and we will start over again, and I'll deal with the boring beginnings as I have done countless times before, and I'll be fine. But you, *you*, will be devastated. You will feel the loss and hurt, and it will press into you for an eternity."

She returned the staff to its original place and stared into Maladaa's black eyes. There was nothing to be seen. She had peered into everything. The remnants of the antilife were fixed within a crystal tomb. The timeline appeared undisturbed by him. She still sensed there was something that she couldn't detect, but whatever it was resisted her understanding. One facet of this scenario was fully understood, however. Irrespective of the reason for Maladaa's backtracking to Pearl, she recognized that he needed to get out of his suit of flesh and beyond this planet before his eroding perspective caused him to create a paradox. Going back to the basics would serve neither of their interests, and she shriveled at the thought of all that would be lost.

"To be clear, the deal is a truce on Pearl. Is this what you seek?" she asked.

Cirrus's golden eyebrows lifted and fell before Maladaa could stop the reaction. "Yes," he replied. "I have no interest in retreading failed ground, but I know how your vimstream works. If it's allowed to grow unchecked, the balance will eventually tip in your favor. These people may be feeding on it at this point in time, but I know you, and I know what you're planning. You will continue to meddle, continue to cheat, and if I let you, you will do something to prevent them from destroying it." He reached out further to his opponent. "So, yes, old friend, let's call a truce here. We'll leave, and they'll destroy themselves as every other sentient species has done, and we'll continue to progress in our respective pursuits."

Baladaa's all-seeing eyes swept across Pearl for what she believed to be the last time. The strange and unique creatures scampered and flew through the wonderful palette of colors before her, and she blessed everything within her power. The impending loss combined with her hesitation, and she nearly rejected the deal. But as she refocused upon her rival, she saw no better option. He meant what he said. She knew if she refused his offer, he would unravel all their work. "Let us," she whispered.

With eyes locked, they stepped toward each other. Their outstretched hands met, and they pulled themselves close. The dark sky and smoky air wiped away, and for a moment, all that could be seen between them was a flickering of black and white. They fell through nothing and everything. All of existence was shifting. What Baladaa had sensed earlier returned sevenfold, and intense regret washed over her.

Their incoherent surroundings found shape and meaning. They were standing in front of a white barn. Gigantic cats were unmoving in the fields. A house stood not far from them. At the foot of the expansive porch's stairs, a girl held the hand of a young boy. Along with everything else, the two children were motionless as they ascended toward the home.

A man with short red hair stood at the top of the stairs. Beside him, a woman with fingerless gloves was bent down in an encouraging pose that appeared to be directed toward the boy. Both adults smiled at the younger set, and the warmth of their love radiated through frozen time. Beyond the couple, in the frame of the home's entrance, another version of Cirrus and the white-haired woman were staring into each other's eyes. One of his hands rested upon her dress's rounded midsection. His expression was that of Baladaa's upon reviewing her creation, while the white-haired woman's was a joy that shone brighter than all understanding.

As if an unseen stone had been thrown at the scene, black cracks formed around Baladaa and Maladaa. "No!" she cried.

Her previous stoicism was breaking with the time and space around them. "What did you do?" she screamed. The nails of the young woman dug into Cirrus's flesh as her grip tightened on his extended hand.

Chunks of reality broke apart and flew out of sight. Darkness began framing them. The grin on Cirrus's face sliced at Baladaa. "There's no need to hold on so tight." Excitement amplified his tone. "We're not done yet. We're going to make one more stop before we leave this place behind." Cirrus's free hand gripped the white-haired woman's, and Maladaa forced Baladaa to step back.

They relived the disorienting experience through flashes of black and white. A musty smell fell over them, and a dim setting surrounded them. They were in a large room with rows of curved wooden benches. Hundreds of candles hung from the ceiling, and vague light revealed the temple's beauty. At the center of the rows of empty benches, upon a stone alter, knelt another version of the white-haired woman. Her hands were clasped, and her attention was turned down to the gray.

"This is it!" Maladaa exclaimed. Cirrus's face became so filled with glee that it lost any ties to the man. Maladaa's black eyes bulged from their alien sockets, and a stretching smile tore at the sides of the ex-MERCENARY soldier's face.

Baladaa watched in horror as a green glow replaced her dance partner's protruding eyes. Cirrus's head snapped back, and a shadow gushed from every orifice on his face. The torrent of darkness carried with it the green light, and the cloud of shadows appeared to glare in Baladaa's direction as it settled not far from her. The shapeless presence pulled in on itself, and the green glow floated toward the upper reaches of the darkness.

Maladaa's eyes were back in their original place, but Cirrus's face remained stretched as bloody tears and red drool trickled over his skin. Maladaa's focus followed Baladaa's to the materializing entity. The black fog solidified into a silhouette that towered over both of them.

The outline developed in to a complete man. His green eyes cast their light throughout the cavernous cathedral. The silver hair, which stretched from his scalp, rested upon a thick master's robe. Fixed against his back, a slender sword rested. He grew a smirk as his stare found Maladaa's.

"Baladaa, old friend, I'd like to introduce you to my son, Aggeroth Wyvern."

Baladaa's grip loosened considerably as she fought to understand what was playing out. "Impossible," she whispered.

Maladaa sighed loudly and made sure to keep a hold on the body that temporarily housed Baladaa. "Your lack of confidence in my abilities is very insulting." The blood that was dripping from Cirrus's eye sockets and the corners of his mouth disintegrated while his disturbingly loose face pulled itself back to its original state. "He's mine, or at least he's as close to being my son as possible. Surely you can sense it by now. This all must be very confusing, so allow me to elucidate. Now that Aggeroth and I are in two places, you perceive my presence times two, right?"

"Yes—"

"When we were sharing the same body, you couldn't sense it because he was made from me!" Maladaa tightened his grip on the young woman's hand, and he started shimmying in place. "Oh, look at that face, Son! She's shocked!" Unrestrained laughter caused him to bend over, and he yanked her down with him. "Now you know how I feel being surrounded by the countless splinters of you," he gasped.

"Imagine how I felt when I found out," Aggeroth said. His tone was ice water.

Maladaa's blazing glee vanished. "Yes, yes, I'm sure your existence has been just awful, Son. All the powers of the anti-life, an existence beyond anything to have ever walked Pearl, handsome, tall—yes, I apologize for orchestrating your creation. I hope that our plans will properly culminate, and you will receive all that I've promised. However, if this is too much of a burden, you needn't oblige me. If you'd rather sip barretinis at a resort on some tropical coast—"

"What is wrong with you?" Aggeroth closely examined Maladaa's eyes. "You're acting strange."

Cirrus's rigid hair loosened, and the spikes of blond bent over one another while a few fell across his forehead. When Maladaa recognized what was happening, the hair snapped straight and pointed to the frozen flames above their heads. "I'm fine!" he shouted. "It's this body. It's broken, but in a good way. Didn't you notice it? Something is missing, or there's something extra, I don't know, but I like it."

"He was one of Vayne's pin cushions," Aggeroth muttered. "It's how he was strong enough—"

Sparkling iridescent threads emerged from the stone floor and began wrapping themselves around Aggeroth's black boots. A layer of clear crystal formed and followed the exploring energy as it crawled up his footwear. When he noticed this, he pulled his feet free from their solidifying position. Crystal shards clattered to the floor and melted into the iridescent energy that had formed them. As soon as they were back to their original state, the threads of light followed with the still emerging others to the man in black.

"Really?" Maladaa exclaimed. He cast a glare at the gathering threads of energy, and they vanished. "While I'm standing right here? You must be scared."

"So many things have changed," she whispered. "How did you do it?" Her defeated tone was music to Maladaa.

"Me?" Maladaa poked a finger at Cirrus's chest. "I didn't do anything. I won't do anything. That was our agreement, remember? We aren't going to be able to come back once we let go. Any alterations to the fabric are and will be owed to…" He finished his thought by pointing to Aggeroth.

The man in black retrieved his sword and shifted his gaze to the kneeling white-haired woman at the center of the room. "I could've stopped him, but I let him do it. I thought the voices would go away. I thought it would die with me, but it is me. This was inevitable, I understand that now."

"Stop being so melodramatic!" Maladaa flared. "Just do as we planned, and we will rule together when the balance is finally tipped."

"Don't listen to him, Aggeroth." Baladaa's tone regained its original composure. "He does not want to rule with anyone. He will cast you aside once you have served your purpose. Your destiny is not written in your origin. Your choices write your future. If you do not wish to suffer, I can help you."

Maladaa turned from the weakening face of the thing he called his son and grabbed the young woman's free hand. "You're not going to stop this," he seethed. His space invaded hers, and the two were surrounded by flashes of black and white.

The stink of the slums returned. They were back where and when they had begun. The moment was frozen, and it wouldn't thaw until the deal was complete. Maladaa released one of the white-haired woman's hands, and he stared at the fallen flowers. They floated up and returned to their original position in front of the young woman.

"Grab them," he ordered.

"No," she retorted.

With confidence, Maladaa bent down toward Baladaa and kissed her. As he did this, he threw the white-haired woman's other hand away, and the flowers again fell to the ground. When the kiss was done, and their lips parted, they were cast into the ether.

Chapter 16

THEY FOUND EACH other at the same time. Lightening flashed in the clear blue sky of his eyes while her dark-green jewels peered into him. An aura of pleasant aromas radiated from her and briefly pushed away the smell of the slums. Her upper lip began to grow cool as the evidence of their kiss met the air.

Thoughts materialized in his mind, and he attempted to fill the gap that would reveal what led to this point. He had been staring at her pink flowers, and now he was leaning into her. His lips were moist, and foreign sweetness lingered in his mouth.

The electric blue eyes were unlike anything she had ever seen. Miniature lightning strikes crisscrossed one another and beckoned her attention like a charm. The emerging blond shadow on his angular jaw framed the face that was causing a tiny ballerina to do pirouettes in her midriff. He had saved her, and he must have taken a kiss for payment. She recalled no hint of an incoming advance, but this fact dwindled from relevance as his presence ensconced her.

He purposefully blinked and pulled back. His search for a subject upon which to seize ended with the sight of the pile of pink flowers that rested on the ground. He dove down to pick them up without a word.

It took a few seconds for her to break from whatever power had hypnotized her. She stared down at the crouching man as he grabbed the flowers and tried to organize them with all the blooms facing the same way. The cluster of spikes atop his head wobbled as he worked, and she fought the urge to touch them.

He looked to her as he stood back up. "You should carry a weapon if you're going to be out, alone at this time. It'd be more effective than…" He presented the pink bouquet.

She accepted the offering. "I sell them," she explained. The words were meeker than expected. "Travelers buy them for their loved ones."

He arched an eyebrow. "Isn't it a little early in the day? It doesn't get busy until Lazla's first light."

She held out the bouquet for him to examine. "These are Rosa's steeples. They bloom at midnight and whither in Lazla's light. I have different flowers for different times of the day."

"Where did you find flowers in the slums?" he asked. The strange blip in his memory nagged at him. "I didn't think even weeds could grow here." He strived to keep his tone casual as he attempted to understand his uncharacteristic action.

Her gaze met his again. "I grow them." A hint of pride crept into her soft tone. "They grow in my backyard."

"Really?" he asked. "You must not live around here." He glanced around at the barren soil.

Her free hand brushed over the top of the bouquet. "Actually, I live on the edge of Division Six, and Lazla's light reaches my land in the early morning." She shrugged. "I'm lucky, I guess." Her eyes fell away again. "People like them. Flowers bring happiness."

"But the soil in the slums…I've heard that the vim reactors are polluting the land for kilometers around Urba."

She grinned. "What's your name?" she asked. After examining the flowers, she plucked one from the rest.

"Cirrus Stark," he responded.

She held out the single flower. "I'm Grace Stillwater."

Apprehensively, he accepted her offering. "I, uh, how much?" he asked.

She sighed. "It's a gift," she explained.

He shook his head, and a spike folded over his left eye. He pushed it back up. "I can't accept it. Not if you're selling them to make a living."

A comfortable pause lasted for a moment. "Fine," she announced. A full smile grew from her grin. "I'll take one shill, and it's yours."

He stared into her as he attempted to solve the puzzle of their familiarity. "Okay," he relented. He reached into one of his blood-red pockets and pulled out a tiny copper octagonal cylinder.

Their skin briefly touched, and a spark snapped at her. "Ouch!" she exclaimed.

"Sorry," he mumbled. "It happens sometimes. I try to keep it under control, but…" He brought the flower to his nose. It smelled fresh. "You're the first girl to give me a flower."

Her smile returned as she dropped the shill into a pocket. As she did this, she rubbed her palm against the soft fabric in an attempt to smother the lingering stinging sensation. "I'm glad I could be your first."

A smirk appeared and vanished on his face within a second. "I'm happy to have made your acquaintance, Ms. Stillwater—"

"Oh, call me Grace. I mean, if you want to. I know MERCENARY has their standards, so if you can't, it's not a big deal. Do you prefer Mr. Stark or Cirrus?"

"I, uh, Cirrus is fine, but I should be on my way. Again, it was nice meeting you, and…" He briefly paused. "I'm sorry for…I don't know why I…"

"Are you on patrol? I didn't think MERCENARY soldiers were still down here. Are you a bodyguard?"

He scratched the back of his head, and a particularly painful spark snapped between his index finger and his scalp. "Something like that," he admitted. His gaze shifted beyond Grace as he attempted to signal that he didn't have time to talk.

She tightened her grip on the cool stems of the flowers and started swaying to draw back his attention. "Do you enjoy it?" she asked.

"What?" He refocused on her.

"Being a MERCENARY soldier—do you enjoy it? I bet you've had some adventures."

"I wouldn't call them adventures."

"Oh?" she pried.

"Ms. Stillwater, I need to—"

"Grace!" she interjected. A forced laugh followed the near-shout. "Please call me Grace."

He caught her eyes with his and nodded. "Grace, I need to be on my way. I have a job to do; people are waiting for me."

She nodded without thinking. "When you're done, maybe we could—"

"I would learn to use and carry a weapon if you're going to be in the streets at this hour." He brushed passed her. A sweet scent rushed to and away from him. "Stay safe, Grace." The words slipped out as he forced himself onward.

After parting ways with her, Cirrus gently placed the flower in a pocket on the inside of his jacket. The familiar bright lights of the train station rested at the end of the road. From there, he would ride to his destination.

Chapter 17

ORYN RUBBED A hand over his face, and emerging short hairs dragged over his skin. Avalanche's atmosphere was quiet on this night, and he was glad to have the tavern almost entirely to himself. Behind the drinktop, Rick Gard was busy polishing mugs as he occasionally glanced up at the electronic display that hung above the ice maker. Oryn had briefly tried paying attention to the fighters who were circling above the frozen water, but the asymmetry of the poor reception prevented his focus from taking hold.

Rick's deep voice rolled over the monotonous chattering that was coming from the electronic display. "You look like someone took a shit in a box, wrapped it up in fancy paper, put a ribbon on it, and then handed it to you on your birthday."

Oryn's stare broke from his half-full mug and found the beefy man. With the thick hair that covered his muscular forearms, and the black beard that hid the lower half of his face, Rick evoked visions of wild animals in Oryn's mind. He summoned a winning smile and raised his mug. "Thanks, Rick. You look like a walf fucked a kameroon, a pup was had, and that pup was you."

"I take that as a compliment, Stillwater."

"As you should, my friend." Oryn sipped from the mug, and the dark beer briefly assaulted his senses.

Rick sprayed the rag with a solution that smelled like kuple flowers and began polishing the drinktop's surface. "Okay, okay, you don't have to talk. It is my job though, to listen, I mean. So, if you change your mind..." he trailed off.

"And here I thought your job was to serve me brown piss water," Oryn jested.

"Hey! Take that back. I made that beer myself. I grew the ingredients in my yard. I took hours preparing them, days combining them; my blood, sweat, and tears are in that beer, damn it!"

"So that's the aftertaste, huh?"

Rick pretended to laugh and snatched the mug away from Oryn. Before an objection could be voiced, he pulled a thin glass from beneath the drinktop and placed it in front of his friend. "All right, ma'am, what kind of fancy girly cocktail should I make for you? How about a violet cactus? Maybe you're into the fun stuff. Let's set you up with a heart of fire, or perhaps we should go for the other extreme and freeze your balls with a polar dream."

"Fuck you, give me back my piss water."

A look of satisfaction filled Rick's face, and he replaced the thin glass with Oryn's mug. "I knew you liked it."

Oryn took another sip and shrugged.

"Come on, man. You're in here every night lately. You sit and nurse on maybe two or three beers over as many hours. I know you want to talk. I'm a pro, I can sense it. Spit it out before it poisons you."

Oryn bit his bottom lip to keep from making another quip about the beer. "Gale is pregnant," he sighed.

Rick let out a hearty laugh and snatched the mug away again. "Congratulations, man! Let me get you a fresh one on the house." He dumped the mug in the sink before filling it back up. "Lulu and I should catch up. Sagacious needs a brother to scare away boys like your son."

Oryn's eyebrows lifted. "What?" he asked.

"I'm joking. Cirrus is a gentleman. I think they have a little thing going. He's over at our place all the time. Occasionally, I'll check in on them, and I gotta tell you, man. I think you've done a good job."

Oryn stifled a laugh and brought the mug to his lips.

"It wasn't a joke. You're a good father. Don't be so worried. The second can't be as hard as the first. You and Gale are more prepared now. You'll be fine. Keep it up though, and you'll be like old man Cid. That ancient fuck has more kids than I have digits. I bet he's got bastards all over the region too."

Oryn winced and drank from his mug again.

Rick noticed the reaction and paused as he attempted to figure out how best to approach the question. "When is your next Urba assignment?" he asked.

"Soon," he sighed.

"Shit, didn't you just get back?"

"Yeah," he muttered.

"And the other MERCENARY soldiers, at the research facility, are fine with you taking another job already?"

Oryn's blood-shot eyes looked up from his mug. "Guarding that place is easy shill. They're more than happy to take the hours." The sharp articulation of his words told Rick to back off.

"I've never been to the big city. I've always wanted to go. Is it true that the businesses there are open all day and all night?"

"Yeah."

"Lulu might throw a fit, but what do you think about me joining you, next time you go?"

"What?" Oryn's voice caught in his throat, and he cleared it with a cough.

"Yeah, I know you'll be on assignment and staying at the base, but I can get a room somewhere, and it's not like I expect you to give me a grand tour. When you have time, you can show me your favorite tavern. Maybe I'll get some ideas, or inspired, or something."

Oryn's tired eyes were now fully open, they stumbled to the large man, and he forced them back to his mug. "You might want to wait until autumn. The, uh, plate can make the slums stink."

"Shit, man, you think I'd stay in the slums? No fucking way. I never get a solo vacation. When I finally do, I'm living the high-life. I'll be staying somewhere in District One, probably above a casino. It's going to be great. What do you think?"

Oryn reached for his face again and teased his stubble. He reluctantly looked to Rick. "Sure, it sounds great," he relented.

The bell above the tavern's entrance jingled. A gush of cool air flooded the tavern, and Rick's focus shifted to the stranger. Most people, upon entering Avalanche, surveyed the establishment. They'd hesitate near the door and look at the décor. Maybe they'd spot an acquaintance before quickly dissolving into the cozy setting.

This man did no such thing. His direction was immediate and purposeful. He cut across the tavern in what seemed to be one long stride. His black robe covered a tall thin frame and concealed his feet as he smoothly made his way toward the friends.

Oryn noticed Rick's soured demeanor, and he looked over his shoulder as the man with the long silver hair approached the drinktop. The smell of charred wood accompanied the stranger, and Oryn coughed into a fist as unseen ash infiltrated his lungs. Glowing green eyes glared down at him, and the questions that were popping into his mind vanished.

"My apologies." The man in black's words fell from his lips like snow.

"What can I get you, sir?" Rick asked. His casual aura had shifted to formal. Oryn noted that his posture was unusually straight, as if the end of a sword was poking the small of his back.

The stranger drummed bony fingers on the drinktop as he appeared to consider his response. "Take a nap, Rick," he said.

Rick dropped to the floor with a thud. Oryn's mouth hung open as he stood and looked over the drinktop. "Rick, what happened? Are you okay?" His speech slurred, and the extent of his drunkenness was realized.

"He's fine, Oryn. He'll wake up in a few hours and tell himself that he's been working too hard. He'll be more relieved that his shill drawer is untouched than anything else."

Oryn felt himself fall back to his stool. "Have we met?" he asked. The glowing green of the man's eyes captured his attention.

A smirk vanished as quickly as it materialized on the smooth face. "Yes, we have, Oryn."

Oryn's hands found their way to his lap, and he frowned. "I'm sorry, I don't—"

The stranger waved off the rest of the sentence. "Yes, I know, you don't remember. Forgive me, Oryn, but you people all say the same thing every time and everywhere I go. I'm sure you can imagine how tiresome it gets."

"I, uh, what?"

An annoyed sigh preceded an intake of breath. "I'm going to need you to focus, Oryn. Are you able to do that?" The green lights that were his eyes pressed into their object of interest.

"Yeah," Oryn mumbled.

"I'm in the midst of weaving a very delicate course of events. It's much more difficult than I thought. To tell the truth, I'm surprised by the challenge. An unseen and undetectable force attempts to pull things along their tried paths. I knew the fabric would have some sort of self-preservation mechanism, but it's beginning to drive me mad. I can change things, but given all that must adjust to accommodate the changes, I'm met with resistance whenever I try. Apparently, just as points further along in the timeline depend on their past, points further back in the timeline depend on their future." He raised one of his skeletal hands, and a look of realization showed from his face. "That's why it's called a fabric."

Oryn nodded.

"Excuse the digression, now that Father is gone, I lack anyone to speak with about such things. It's almost enough for me to reconsider my plans for him."

Oryn nodded again.

"Enough of that. Let's not waste any more time. Oryn, your oldest son is in danger, and he will require your help."

Oryn blinked as his thoughts stumbled over one another. "Cirrus is my only son," he murmured.

Two bony fingers pointed to the glowing eyes. "Focus, Oryn. I want you to stay focused."

"Okay."

"The danger will come in the form of a young woman, decades from now. If we allow circumstances to go unchecked, she will destroy that which makes him who he is. We must stop her to save him."

"How?"

The glowing eyes brightened as the man in black reviewed the pertinent moments. So many different strings needed to be pulled, and the fabric would resist each adjustment. He wished to rain fire down upon the girl and her mother before they left Farron, but he knew any attempt would end up being a waste of time, given all that would need to readjust.

"I will try to arrange her mother's death earlier in her life for it is familial knowledge that is Cirrus's greatest danger. My goal is to sever her from her roots before she becomes knowledgeable of the white essenia's capabilities. If I can manage it, she will be more easily guided in a favorable direction."

"White essenia?" Oryn asked.

"Don't worry about it, Cirrus will be protected from it. The threat to him is the young woman."

Oryn nodded.

"As I was saying, whenever the girl is orphaned, she will require a home. You and Emma will raise her. You will influence and guide her as I instruct."

Oryn blinked as thoughts rushed to his mind. "Emma and I will raise her?"

"Yes, she has always wanted a child, but she cannot have one, correct?"

"Yeah, but—" he began.

The glow of the green eyes focused on their target and intensified. "It is everything she has ever wanted, Oryn. To be a mother and wife, to live with you and serve you. Surely, you won't deny her, will you?"

The brightness of the stranger's eyes was too intense, and Oryn looked away. As he did, thoughts of Cirrus, Gale, and the baby that would arrive came to mind. "I can't leave them," he whispered. "I don't want to hurt Emma. I want her to be happy, but—"

"Oh! All the gold in all the universe I'd pay to not have to deal with you pests. Every time I work out a perfect chain of events, one of you creatures screws it up! I can't control everything, Oryn. I can't force you disgusting animals to do what is best. All I can do is point and nudge. And do you take the bait? Do you grab what you want—what is best for everyone? *NO!*"

"I'm sorry—"

"He's sorry! I hand him everything, offer to save his son, and he's sorry that he can't accept my generosity," the man in black screamed. He began furiously nodding. His bony hands found his silver hair, and he steadied the movement.

"I'll figure it out, *again*. Don't you worry, Oryn. Your stupid selfishness won't derail me. I'll taste her blood and crush that fucking crystal. And when I'm done, when the Sentinels are gone, and I have free reign, I will devour the planet. Every spec of vim will become part of me, and I will be reborn as this wretched realm's alpha and omega."

Chapter 18

"You look…different," Julie commented. She stifled a giggle.

Dash awkwardly bent down and sat next to her after he exited the café's restroom. "It's too small," he breathed. His face was flushed and stressed.

"It'll stretch," Cirrus assured him.

"Will mine shrink?" Sagacious asked. "My sleeves are way too long." She lifted her arms for the other five at the table to see. The ends of the MERCENARY uniform's sleeves reached her fingers.

"I think red is your color," Wells commented. He winked at her.

"Give it a rest," Brack grunted. He was hunched over their table staring at the screen on his computer. "Sagacious wants a man who doesn't need a step stool to reach the top shelf."

"I'd rather be on the smaller side than a giant freak!" Wells snapped.

"Boys!" Sagacious interrupted. "Now's not the time."

Cirrus grabbed one of her wrists and rolled up the long sleeve. "There," he stated.

"Thanks," she responded. His attitude worried her.

"What if I unclasp it? I have an undershirt on," Dash suggested.

"You should keep it clasped," Cirrus responded. "Think of it as armor."

"Really?" Sagacious asked. She felt the material between her fingers.

"Ruby araneid fur is woven into fabric and used for all MERCENARY uniforms. They're not impenetrable, but they'll keep most blades from getting to you and absorb the blow of blunt weapons," Cirrus explained.

"What!" Sagacious exclaimed. "That's disgusting. Please tell me you're joking." She stared at her uniform.

"That's gross," Julie agreed. She broke off a piece of her scone and popped it into her mouth. Her muffled speech became barely audible. "You do look good though."

"I'm not joking," Cirrus said.

"MERCENARY soldiers are nasty," Dash said. He rubbed the red jacket that strained against his torso. "Back in the Quartz Mountains, every spring, my hometown would get infested by hordes of newly hatched ruby araneids." He held up his large hands and made a circle by touching the tips of his thumbs and his forefingers to illustrate the size of the baby spiders.

"They terrified Fran. She would keep Cindy inside the house until the araneids migrated to the desert." Dash smiled warmly as he picked at his cookie. "Cindy would go watch them from the living room window. She was fearless." Dash's words broke, and he diverted his glassy eyes from the group.

Cirrus was about to ask for an explanation, but Sagacious caught his attention. "Not now," she mouthed.

"Anything with eight legs is gross," Brack mumbled.

"Dash, you can unclasp it if you want. But if you're attacked, you'll be sorry," Cirrus said.

"Is it bulletproof?" Wells asked. He reached below the table and pulled up the gun that had been strapped to his waist. "I know you told me this would be useless, but I'm a pretty decent shot."

Cirrus sighed. "No, MERCENARY uniforms aren't bulletproof, but they don't need to be."

"What do you mean?" Wells asked.

"Every MERCENARY soldier carries at least one essenia orb. If the bearer of the orb forms a bond with it, it will protect him or her by means of a will field, and you can bet that any soldiers who are assigned to guard a reactor have accomplished that."

"Oh, I think I've heard of will fields," Julie interjected.

"Will fields protect people from attacks and threats that lack will to back them up," Cirrus explained.

The table went silent for a few seconds.

"I don't get it," Wells said. "When I shoot at someone, there is a will to hit my target. How can an attack lack will?"

"Will comes from a being's vim. Anything touched by a person is influenced by that person's will. Once an object loses contact with a person, the relationship between the person's will and the object disappears. Will may begin an action, but physical laws can carry it through to completion.

"A will field is an extension of a person's vim. The essenia projects the person's vim outward. Threats that lack will are blocked by the field. But if an individual attacks someone, who's protected by a will field, whether it's with a sword, baton, their own fists, or any weapon that stays connected to the attacker, their wills nullify each other and contact can be made."

Wells raised his gun and aimed at Cirrus's head. "So, if I fired at you, you're saying your little round crystal will protect you?"

"Put that thing away," Brack said. He glanced up from his computer. "You're not scaring anyone."

"What about those of us who don't have essenia?" Sagacious asked. "What if the MERCENARY soldiers guarding the reactors have guns?"

"I doubt that will be the case," Cirrus answered. "Megacorp would never trust the task of guarding a vim reactor to artillery specialists. They're usually used for crowd control or intimidation."

"Will the guards be able to do mystics?" Dash asked. "I don't want to burst into flames like that roglop."

"I wouldn't be surprised if they turn out to be advanced in both power and technique if there are only two of them guarding the reactor." Cirrus reached into his pack and pulled out three rings. They showed a clean reflection. He slipped one of the smooth bands over the middle finger of his left hand.

"Specula?" Sagacious gasped. "Cirrus, if we're caught with specula rings, they'll lock us up and throw away the keys." As she said this, she slid a ring on and marveled at its reflective quality.

Julie bent over and admired Dash's new ring. "I'm jealous, I've never received jewelry from a man."

Dash gently pushed her face back. "Sagacious, if we're punished for anything, it's not going to be for having specula." He shoved the ring onto his left little finger. "These will deflect mystics, right?"

"Yeah," Cirrus answered. "Mystics are deflected by anything with specula on or around it. It's something that all MERCENARY soldiers wear. There's a good chance that I won't be able to use mystics on the guards."

"We'll be able to take them," Dash said.

"How can you perform mystics when you're wearing specula?" Sagacious asked.

"Specula deflects mystics—not will. Will is the energy responsible for creating mystics from vim. When mystics are performed, the person responsible wills their essenia to create mystics. Once the energy transforms, it is deflected by specula." Cirrus explained.

"Keep in mind that specula deflects all mystics," he continued. "If either of you are injured, the ring will need to come off before I can heal you."

"But if we take off the ring, they will be able to fry us?" Dash asked.

Cirrus nodded. "Avoid being injured."

The distance between the café and Reactor Seven was short, but their travel time seemed to stretch. The nearly constant wind atop the plate brushed against the backs of the six as they walked down the metal pathway. Their destination poked into the black sky and pointed to hundreds of loose diamonds that covered the dark velvet. The view was breathtaking for those who called the slums home.

The sharp and daunting crescent of Rosa hung in the opposite direction of the tower. Its ruddy glow shone upon the reactor. The building's expansive windows reflected its soft light.

Cirrus couldn't dismiss the unsettling absence of security. There was a gate at the front, but it was wide open. No one sat in the harpeia's nest that overlooked it. Why was the security so relaxed? More questions rushed through his mind as he scanned the site.

"It's so c-cold up here," Julie chattered. She and Cirrus were in a loose line behind Brack and Wells. They were being led by Sagacious and Dash.

"Yeah, it's cooler up here," Cirrus responded. His gaze found hers. "There's always a breeze, but the wind isn't like this all around the plate." He pointed beyond the reactor. "There aren't barriers around any of the reactors' edges."

Julie hugged herself. Her unflattering short-sleeved shirt did little to keep her warm. "Why?" she asked. The word escaped through her clenched teeth.

"I'm not sure..." Cirrus trailed off as he thought about it. "Megacorp might see it as a display of power. I suppose it could be considered a form of advertising." He shrugged playfully. "It's possible that the executives just want an unobstructed view."

"That's c-c-crazy."

Cirrus rolled his eyes. "Do you want my jacket? I gave Dash and Sagacious my spare uniforms and specula rings because they volunteered to take on any threats. I didn't consider—"

She shook her head and smiled. "No, you're r-right. I'm not much help in a fight. Keep your jacket on, I want my bodyguard to be safe."

He attempted to return the smile but was unsure if he was successful. Her kind face prodded at his frosted heart. He diverted his attention and focused on the intimidating edifice.

Chapter 19

THE DARK ROOM pulsed with music as spinning balls flickered and rolled across the ceiling. The air was thick with the evidence of bodies on the eighty-fourth floor of Megacorp's headquarters; an invisible blanket wrapped Verdel Xing in heavy humidity. Green liquid in his crystal glass glowed whenever one of the balls of light passed above him, and the realization that he was beginning to get lost in the turtle's paradise encroached upon him.

Elena Cayt found a seat next to him and signaled the boy behind the drinktop. The black-haired youth rolled his eyes and sauntered toward her. "Yeah?" he asked.

She reached across the surface and gripped the front of the boy's shirt. With a swift yank, she pulled him halfway over the drinktop. When she managed to get one of his ears near her glossy lips, she spoke. "Show some respect," she demanded. Her grip loosened, and she allowed him to look at her again. A feigned smile formed.

"I-I'm sorry," he responded.

She didn't hear the words, but the eyes of the boy yielded what she sought. "Give me a polar dream." He nodded and produced a bottle of blue liquid from beneath the drinktop. Wisps of cold air fell from the bottle as frost spread on the outside of the receiving glass.

"Was that performance for me?" Verdel asked. He smirked, and the scar across his left cheek distorted. "You already have the job, Elena."

Blood rushed to her face. "No, that's just how I handle myself."

He winked and nodded as his only hand picked up his glass. The pungent aroma poked into his nostrils while he sipped the bitter liquid. Embers within his chest reignited as the green accelerant splashed over them. Before he returned the turtle's paradise to its place, he felt reality further smudge. The lights above him were now dancing, and the previously uncomfortable humidity caused him to feel a sense of warm nirvana.

"I've always wanted to be a clandestine," she said.

He forced his gaze to settle on her. "We're going to have to get you out of that uniform."

"Excuse me?" She assumed she had misheard him over the relentless music that was thumping from the walls.

He motioned to the red fabric that covered her body. "Clandestines don't wear *that*." He hiccupped and closed his eyes for a moment. When he reopened them, he noticed something else. "And that hair of yours is too long. I want it cut tomorrow. It shouldn't touch your shoulders."

She reached for the lengthy, single braid. "It wasn't a problem in first class."

Verdel began to respond when he felt someone grip his shoulders from behind. "Xing! I'm glad you could make it." He broke eye contact with Elena and turned to the owner of the claw-like hands.

Dane Kefka's white suit and pallid face absorbed the shifting colors of the room. His rust red hair was slicked back with a product that added a polished quality. Coupled with an intense stare, he reminded Verdel of sand serpents. "Thank you for inviting us, Mr. Kefka."

"Of course, of course, you and the rest of the clandestines are always invited." Dane's smile revealed a mouthful of perfect teeth. His attention found Elena and he winked. "You must be the new girl."

"Yes, sir," she said. A hand extended toward the vice president of Megacorp.

He stared at her for a moment before taking her offering and kissing the back of it. "It is a pleasure with no comparison, fair lady."

She mirrored his playful smirk and tone. "The pleasure is surely mine, kind sir."

He released Elena's hand and turned back to Verdel. "I have a good feeling about this one, Xing. Is she all set for the White Project?"

Verdel put down his now empty glass. "This was her first day, sir." He balled his fists and struggled to control his breathing as he tried to convince himself that Dane Kefka was not a sand serpent.

"Well, she'll have a busy second day, won't she?"

Verdel strained to translate the hissing into whatever words that were being spoken. His superior's large grin flashed teeth that seemed to stretch, and he nodded while hoping the monster wouldn't devour him.

"I think someone may be lost in the turtle's paradise," Dane said. He swooped down and put his face in front of Verdel's. "I can see into you, my friend. You're frightened. What's wrong, Xing? Has the turtle led you astray?" As he spoke he swayed back and forth.

A cackle escaped Elena, and Verdel's reddening eyes broke from Dane's glare. "You're as bad as they say," she said.

Dane shifted toward her and stared into her. His teeth disappeared, and his smile weakened. "Oh, you're no fun. Why haven't you joined them? Where's your drink?" He spotted the now cloudy crystal glass. "A polar dream, I see. It's always enjoyable to meet another person who appreciates what the cold has to offer. Have you ever been to the Far North, fair Elena?"

Bemused by his attention, she shook her head.

"There is no place colder on Pearl. There are walls of blue ice and endless dunes of powdery snow. It is said that the mountains have caves that are rich with raw and rare essenia."

Elena grabbed the frosty glass and sipped a bit of the liquid. A chill raced through her, and she shivered. "It sounds beautiful. Maybe I'll charter a flight someday."

"You don't want to do that." His tone taunted her. "There are creatures up there that make sand serpents look like boopuffs." He stifled a laugh as his eyes briefly darted back to

Verdel. The man appeared to be on the edge of unconsciousness as he hunched over the drinktop.

"That's where the star fell, right?" she asked. "I remember learning about it in school. Apparently, when it crashed into the planet, it threw up dirt and dust that blocked Lazla's light for decades. They say it caused a winter that lasted years."

Dane nodded and grabbed the cold glass from her. "From the void, it fell. Air screamed as the stone chamber slammed into frozen ground. With an explosion that rocked every being on Pearl, devastation raced across the land. The antilife devoured without hesitation, and life attempted to hide from its all-seeing eyes."

Surprised by his confiscation of her drink, she forgot her place. "Did you just quote a holy text? I didn't realize I was speaking with a believer."

With a swift and confident movement, he swallowed the polar dream. The thick base of the crystal glass met the hard surface of the drinktop again before his unforgiving grip yanked her up. His icy touch pressed into her flesh, and for a moment, she forgot her training. Her body acquiesced to his forceful guidance, and her feminine aspects shut down any objections. He pulled her close, and his frigid fingers found her hands. She met his copper-colored stare and felt cold air flow as he exhaled.

"I-I'm sorry," she barely managed.

He led her to the center of the floor as those who surrounded them parted and cleared a path. He guided her in a slow dance as lyrics flowed into her.

I will come to you,
As close as I want,
Close enough for me,
To feel your heartbeat,
I stay and whisper,
How I love your eyes...

"All was dark and cold for many seasons," Dane said. His wintery breath hit her neck, and he smiled as she cringed. "The people of Pearl prepared for death to come their way. When hope was nearly lost, and the end was thought to be near, the Sentinels sent forth their strongest warrior. With hair as white as snow and eyes like jewels, she used the planet's lifeblood—"

The music abruptly stopped, and silence filled the eighty-fourth floor of Megacorp's headquarters. Dane's tight grip on Elena loosened, and she exchanged unknowing glances with those around them. His mouth parted, and fascination filled his face.

"Is it working?" A woman, with an impatient tone, broadcast from every corner.

"Yeah, you're live," answered a distant male voice.

"This message is to Megacorp from WAVE—"

The icicles that were Dane's fingers closed over one of Elena's wrists, and they hurried to the elevators near the back of the large room.

"Who is that?" she asked. "Is this a party game? I've heard of your—"

"Stop talking," he interrupted. He smashed the elevators' button and checked to see how many floors it needed to travel to reach them. "We don't have much time. I'm going to give you your first order as a clandestine, and you will follow it without question. Nod if you understand."

Elena restrained her tongue and forced a nod. The woman who had interrupted the music was still speaking, but it was difficult to make any sense of her words. Dane's intense stare pressed into her. An image flashed across her mind of his jaw unhinging. Extending fangs accompanied his almost orange eyes.

"When you exit the building, you will see a white chocorod. You will get in it, and it will take you to Reactor Seven. A terrorist is threatening to bomb the reactor, and you will be the first to intercept her. It is of upmost importance that you eliminate her. If you do, I can promise you my gratitude and a ten percent bonus on top of whatever you will receive for the mission."

Elena watched the elevator doors slide open as Dane stepped aside. He motioned for her to get in. "How do you know—" she began.

"That's none of your business," he snapped. "Go, now!"

"My whip, I need my weapon." The words dropped from her mouth as she felt herself move into the elevator.

"It's waiting for you in the chocorod."

She opened her mouth to ask another question, but she stopped herself as she noticed the ferocity emanating from his face. She slapped the button for the lobby and wished for the doors to separate them.

Chapter 20

AT FIRST, IT appeared to Cirrus that the expansive room beyond the glass was vacant. This notion vanished when a petite woman dressed in MERCENARY red came into view. Her muddy-brown hair had occasional strands of gray. Despite her youthful skin, she appeared to be middle-aged. She yanked on one of the transparent doors that separated her and the group. The weight of the door seemed great as she shifted her entire body to pry it open. Once the entranceway splintered, she slipped out of the building and into the cool air.

"Hello there," she drawled. "How may I help you?" Her accent was thick and dripped with a Great Glacier twang.

"Hello," Cirrus responded. He squeezed between the bodies to get to the front of the group. "I'm here on behalf of Division Seven's manager in chief, Eden Mecia. Madam Mecia has ordered immediate maintenance on Reactor Seven's core. I'm escorting the top core technician in Urba." He gestured to Julie. "The reactor's output is low, and Madam Mecia wants it back to standard levels by Lazla's first light. The notification should have been forwarded to your supervisor."

The woman's welcoming smile cracked. "Oh," she said. She retrieved a fist-sized electronic device from her jacket pocket and ran her fingers across its surface. "I haven't received…" Her thought blew away in the wind. "That's strange," she mumbled. "My link to HQ is down."

"Right, well, these two," he said, gesturing to Sagacious and Dash, "are escorting network techs." He briefly met Sagacious's eyes. "I believe this site's hub is malfunctioning," he finished.

Sagacious's tone was rushed and nervous. "The, uh, head office is reporting that the site's network connection is phasing in and out." The answer came from patchy memories of listening to Brack and Wells, and she wasn't sure if it made any sense.

"Oh my!" The woman's vowels stretched. "Well, thank you for coming at such an early hour! My name is Hilda. Come in, come in, it's chilly out here." With great effort, she pulled open the door. "Braver, have you received any notice of problems with our network connection or the core's output?" Her thick accent shot through the large and nearly hollow lobby.

"No…" responded a throaty and tired voice. A curved desk, not far from the entrance, held within it an aged man. His face poked out from behind an electronic display.

Brack stepped forward. "Urba's central hub was recently updated with a new patch. The update allows for improvements to the network's security, but as it turns out, each site's hub needs an onsite installation. Otherwise, every time the central hub's encryption rolls over, any site that hasn't been updated will have an eighty-seven-point five percent chance of losing connection to the network. It rolls over every three hours. Since we used the sites' original keys as our framework, there's a twelve-point five percent chance that the rollover will involve Site Seven's original key." The words came from the large man in an uninterrupted stream. "Basically, you wouldn't have known there was a problem until there was a problem. It was an oversight by the geniuses on the day shift."

Cirrus wondered if Black's explanation was plausible enough to stand up to a knowledgeable mind. Whether or not it made sense, he was impressed. The large man oozed self-confidence.

Braver's eyes were tired, his brows lifted, and his forehead became fixed with hills and valleys of pale skin. "I've never heard of technicians coming at this hour. Coming here, without prior notification from higher authority, is a breach of protocol. You soldiers are lacking any medallions, which means you all are from entry class…"

Cirrus's attention jumped from the old man to the thin woman and back again. Before arriving, he had imagined that the reactor's MERCENARY soldiers would be formidable and assumed that they would have no trouble with Sagacious and Dash. Now, however, a realization was coming into focus. A challenge to WAVE would require skill and strength, and if the pair of soldiers was as inadequate in battle as he assumed, they would fall to the terrorists. He was still weak in mind and spirit, and Dash's physique made him hesitant to challenge it without proper assistance. If Hilda and Braver fell, he knew that Sagacious wouldn't have the heart to see him die at the hands of her comrades. He'd have to face her judgmental words and accusing stare, and being forced to experience the emotions that would follow was more daunting than anything else.

"With all due respect," Cirrus interjected, "I'm here on behalf of Division Seven's manager in chief. I don't want to be here; I'm just doing my job. If you want to deny us access, that's fine, but you will be the one who will be held responsible."

"Yeah!" Dash interjected. "And, uh, the execs at…the head office are going to blitz you into nothing if the network thing isn't fixed, like, right now."

Braver sighed, and his attention returned to the electronic display. "Fine, do whatever you want. Back in my day, we had respect for protocol…" His voice faded, and he began muttering to himself.

Hilda took a step closer to Cirrus and the others. "I am so sorry, y'all," she whispered. "Braver's not real friendly around this time."

Cirrus nodded. "I don't blame him." He paused. "We should probably get started." His speech slowed, and for the first time, his poise faltered. "Would you, please, show us to the core?" He motioned to Julie again. She curtsied awkwardly beneath her heavy brown pack.

"Oh, you should be able to find it." Hilda let out a delicate laugh. "Braver and I aren't supposed to separate, and we have to stay at our post." She pointed to the back of the large lobby. "It's near the end of that hallway. At the elevator, go to level two. You should be able to find your way from there."

The hallway was long and windowless. His steps felt short. When he noticed the array of lenses hanging from the ceiling, he realized why Hilda was so comfortable allowing him and Julie to roam freely.

As they moved deeper into the reactor, the hair over his body stiffened. A fizzling static buzzed in his ears. His eyes watered as he imagined the constant electrical storm intensifying within his irises.

After the elevator doors closed behind them, Cirrus felt safe talking. "There are lenses all over this place, but I don't think we need to worry about them overhearing us. If they are equipped with microphones, I doubt the audio is listened to live."

"You were great back there," she gushed. Her pack shifted as she gripped the tan straps at her shoulders.

He looked down at her. "It was a lot easier than I thought," he admitted.

The white doors slid open. "I considered taking them down, but going on offense so early might have derailed our chances of success. I didn't see his weapon, but she's carrying truncheons on her hips. If Sagacious and Dash can avoid being smacked in the face, their uniforms will protect them from her..." His voice faded as they made their way into the second level.

As with the first level, the second level was mostly empty. Dividing walls were nonexistent; it appeared to be dedicated to one cavernous room. A desk, which matched the polished surface of the floor in color and reflective shine, stretched in a semicircle around much of the immense area. Dozens of screens were embedded in the elevated surface; many were dark, while others were alive with information.

At the opposite end of the large room, the second level's landscape warped into a hill as different-colored wires and metal tubes replaced the floor. At its apex, a thick stream of glowing vim flowed into free space before disappearing into an aperture in the ceiling. Cirrus stared at the reverse waterfall of energy and marveled at its iridescent quality. The color of the flowing vim shifted so fast that his mind barely had time to register the changes.

A metal ring moved up and down around the flowing energy. The speed of the ring's movement varied. As it floated up and fell down, it erratically turned in alternating directions. After his eyes adjusted to the brightness of the vim, he was able to see specks of material shooting to and from the ring.

Julie craned her neck as she followed Cirrus. "Wow," she breathed. "Is that vim?"

"Yeah," he responded. His eyes were fixed on the core. "Come on, you should probably get started." He motioned her forward. An unseen force threatened to pull him close to the reverse cascade of light. Its beauty was entrancing.

The hairs of his eyebrows stood on end, and adrenaline flooded his body. He wanted to jump into the rushing light. An internal voice screamed through his other thoughts.

"Cirrus!" Julie gasped. She stared into his eyes. "Are you okay? Can you see me?"

"I'm fine," he spat. "Do whatever you need to do."

She forced herself to look elsewhere and made her way to the reactor's core. After she made sure the canister was secured between two bundles of wires, she pulled an electronic device from a pocket in her baggy pants. A red button on the device's screen glowed from its face.

Cirrus broke his focus on the vim. "Do you think thirty minutes will be enough time?" he asked.

She peeked up from the small screen and hesitated before responding. "It'll have to be," she answered. Dread dripped from her. She let out a shaking sigh and pressed the button. Redness expanded to fill the screen. At its center, yellow digits began counting down.

Chapter 21

DASH DROPPED A log on the charred remnants of wood. Sparks and smoke gushed from the fire pit as he jumped back. With no shirt on, the burst of fiery debris threatened his exposed torso. He watched as the glowing bits of hot ash rose into the dark of the early morning. Their brief light vanished before his eyes, and he breathed a sigh of relief.

"There he is, folks. The last hope of Pearl. He may not look like the leaders you've heard about. His body may resemble that of a prepubescent girl. He may not be conventionally smart. But none of that matters, damn it. He has heart. He has courage. And he has that incredibly attractive, stunningly witty, modest sidekick. Yes, the odds are against them, but math isn't their strong suit."

Dash looked to Lucius as he wiped sweat from his face. "Are you done?" he asked.

Lucius tightened his robe as he considered the question. "History is full of little guys, like Dash, who went up against huge opponents. Sure, most of them were flattened before they could pull their weapons, but some of them got lucky. Come on, folks: join our cause and fight the good fight against Megacorp!"

"I hope you have something better than that," Dash said. He began circling the flames. As he neared and passed Lucius, he rubbed his nose. The worms from the frycedust were driving him mad with their wriggling.

"Don't worry, fearless leader. I'm just providing comedic relief in this far too serious tale. Without the levity I provide, where would you be? I'll tell you where: You'd be shivering in front of this fire, alone and depressed while blaming yourself for the town's woes."

Dash exhaled through his nose and wiped more sweat from his face. "It is my fault—"

Lucius raised both arms and briefly stood. "Stop, no, don't even think about starting with the brooding. I cannot stand that shit. Every fucking story has a boring protagonist who is just so magnanimous that he feels as if he alone must carry the burden of responsibility for whatever plight the plot entails. It's lazy and predictable, and I'm not going to let the author of my tale lean on such an unappealing trope."

"What are you talking about?" Dash stopped pacing and covered one nostril with a finger before forcefully blowing. He moaned as he began to move again. "By all holy light, how do you guys snort this shit every day?"

"Every day? Maybe when I was a teenager. To tell you the truth, I'll partake maybe once a month if that. The only reason I keep it on me is for if I meet someone. I figured there will be some potential in Peak Point. Maybe there's a handsome stranger in the city who has never tried frycedust but is looking to experiment. All of a sudden, I go from a seven to a nine."

Dash forced incredulity into his words. "A seven?"

"Hey! I don't appreciate your tone, Mayor Black. I'm gorgeous with the personality of an ugly girl. Sure, I may not be as wealthy as I once was, but I don't need anyone in my life who is there for the amount of shill in my bank account."

Dash fell to his knees and began sobbing. "I'm s-s-sorry, Lucius," he blubbered. "You're going out of business, most of the town is out of work. It's all my fault."

Lucius leaned over to Dash and patted his head. "No one blames you, and what did I just say, Dash? We're not doing the brooding scene. Now, stand up, and walk off those worms."

"I can't!" he cried. As if someone pushed him over, Dash collapsed to one side and curled into a fetal position.

"Look at you, Dash. You're sweaty, shirtless, crying, curled up in a ball; all you need is to be surrounded by cake, and you're me four years ago. Remember when Kimakka dumped me? Now, that was something to be upset about."

"What am I going to do?" Dash moaned. "Even if we can convince people at Peak Point to join our resistance, Quartz Mountains is still—" His words drowned in his sobs.

"Still what?" Lucius demanded. "The town is still there. All the people still live in it. Just because my mines are shuttered doesn't mean Quartz Mountains is doomed. Do you remember what you asked me in the elevator when we were on our way to meet those cretins from Megacorp?"

Dash's tears subsided as he tried to remember.

"You, more or less, asked if people would lose their jobs if mining became more efficient," Lucius prodded.

"Oh yeah," he breathed. "So?"

"Do you remember what I told you?" Lucius pressed.

Dash paused. "You said new jobs would replace old ones."

"Right, and that general principle still holds true, even in the absence of my mines. If people are in Quartz Mountains, there are demands for goods and services. Anyone who is in search of a job need only ask himself how best to provide value to others. Who knows, the absence of mining jobs may be the best thing to ever happen to the town. Creativity will be spurred as people search for ways to satisfy others."

Dash wiped wetness from his face, and he pushed himself upright. His eyes were drawn to the distant horizon where the first streaks of Lazla's light were beginning to stretch across the indigo sky. From his nostrils, four tiny worms dropped to the dirt. A euphoria accompanied their absence. A calm smile emerged on his face.

"Look, you're a mommy!" Lucius pointed to the rapidly growing worms.

"Gross, gross, gross!" He began picking and pawing at his nose.

"Oh, stop it." Lucius suppressed an urge to laugh. "They're all out. You'd know if there were any left. See how big they are already? Keep an eye on them, they'll start spinning their cocoons soon."

Dash blinked slowly as bliss wrapped around him. He wanted nothing more than to be still and watch Lazla's rise. As his fever subsided, and the early morning's chill seeped into him, he began to shiver.

"You are such a mess," Lucius muttered. He found a thin blanket and wrapped it around his friend. "My jokes aren't all vaegah shit. I mean, I think what you're doing, what we're doing, and what the town is doing will be talked about hundreds of years from now. Historians will cite us as the beginning of the end of Megacorp."

"Yeah," Dash breathed. The blues and pinks of the morning were beginning to spread over their darker background. The few clouds overhead were illuminating with Lazla's light, and the exquisiteness of it all was multiplied by the chemicals that the worms had injected into him.

"Maybe they will make statues of us? If they do, I hope the sculptors make my nose smaller. And, if you're lucky, they'll put some muscle on you."

As if ink had been spilled on the beautiful scene before him, smoke began billowing into the pastel portrait from a distant source. Dash stared at the stain in the sky. He knew it was out of place; he knew that it was coming from the direction of Quartz Mountains, but he couldn't react. All he could do was feel the pleasant ecstasy that was increasing in intensity.

"I'm sure it's customary for such things. There's no way those warriors, who fought the antilife, were that buff. Like, a thousand years ago men had access to the nutritional and fitness information to look like that. They didn't have health markets back then, right? Where'd they get all the protein? I mean, I know they hunted, but you have to eat a lot of calories to end up with a body like that."

"Lucius…" Dash mumbled.

"Do you remember, when we took that fieldtrip, to the museum in Doelay, all the art dedicated to the Sentinels? I had the biggest crush on the warrior prince. I used to fantasize about waking up back in that era. Yeah, I know an extraterrestrial monster was wreaking havoc and everything, but all the paintings and sculptures made him out to be so dreamy."

"Look…" Dash's heavy tongue was useless.

"I so wanted to be the daughter of Pearl. She came from nowhere, saved the planet, and snagged the warrior prince. Oh, what was his name? I can't believe I forgot it. Anyway, I refuse to accept that they looked like that. It would be too unfair."

"Smoke!" The word popped out of Dash, and its annunciation shocked his sedated body. His head became heavy, and it tilted toward the ground. The worms were now turquoise cocoons. His stomach turned.

"What?" Lucius asked. "Why don't we get you in your tent? The best way to get the most out of the high is to just lay down. Otherwise, you'll just be sitting, hunched over and probably drooling all over yourself for hours."

"No," Dash moaned.

"I know, I know, you don't want to move. Lucky for you, I'm a pro at picking men up and getting them into bed." Lucius scooped up Dash.

With his field of vision again facing the smoke in the distance, the young husband, father, and mayor of Quartz Mountains felt tears drip from his eyes.

Lucius placed his friend in what he thought was a comfortable position and covered him with the thin blanket. "I know I joke about you being scrawny, but seriously, I have more trouble picking up my laundry. You should think about, you know, making some gains."

Lucius ducked out of Dash's tent. Free of distractions, the dark smudge in the direction of Quartz Mountains was immediately noticed. He squinted as he examined it. Possibilities ran through his mind, but all the minor explanations were dismissed as he began to comprehend the amount of smoke that was pouring into the morning sky.

He opened his mouth to say something to Dash but realized that his friend would be unable to do anything but worry. It had taken six hours to make it this far, but he knew Garnet could cut that time in half if he pushed her. He hastily replaced his robe with clothes. His eyes remained fixed on the ominous sign.

"Garnet!" he yelled.

Dash heard the utterance and the following sound of his friend leaving on his vaegah. With nothing to do but stare at the gray interior of his tent and think, his mind conjured explanations for what he had seen. The most probable scenario, he figured, was that another fire had started at Tantal's. Decades ago, the diner had burned to the ground. Smoke had been everywhere. The people of Quartz Mountains had helped the owners rebuild. They would do it again, he told himself.

Dash hadn't considered his weight when he prepared his line of frycedust. His sedation was much deeper and longer than he had expected. Eventually, he drifted into unconsciousness, and he didn't float from darkness until Lazla was again rising.

When his eyes opened, he slowly sat up. He hadn't moved since the previous morning, and his stiff joints and muscles attested to this fact.

He stretched his legs before nearly rolling out of his tent. As he reached for the canvas of colors above his head and groaned away the sleep, he looked around for Lucius. His friend wasn't there. Garnet was gone too. The sack of vaegah food was torn open, and pellets surrounded Sparro.

"Hey!" he shouted.

The gigantic cat's eyes opened slightly, and he sighed in response.

"What the fuck, Sparro? You didn't need to tear into the bag. Next time, if you want food in the middle of the night, just wake me up. I know you know how to do that."

Sparro stared at Dash for a moment before dismissively walking past him and toward the fire pit. As he sat, his powerful tail slammed against the cold ashes.

"Quit looking at me like that. You know I hate that. You're not smarter than me. You're not better than me."

Four turquoise fryceflies fluttered from out of sight and began circling Dash's head. He swatted at them and ducked. Slowly, he began to recall what had been forgotten. He reached for his nose and rubbed it, while his other hand nervously scratched his chest.

He looked in the direction of Quartz Mountains. There was no sign of smoke. He told himself that was a good thing. His feet carried him back to his tent, and he numbly found a shirt and pants. No thoughts emerged. He wouldn't let them.

"We need to go back," he mumbled. Sparro bowed, and Dash put the saddle in place before mounting him. Their tents remained up, and most of their things hadn't been packed, but none of this registered in Dash's mind. He refused to start thinking. There was a part of him that knew, if he started sifting through his thoughts, he'd regret it.

Sparro moved unusually fast over the terrain. The speed was unsolicited, and Dash began wondering why the vaegah was rushing. This developing thought was smothered not long after it originated, and he allowed the gigantic cat to do what it willed. He attempted to marvel at the beauty of the morning. He told himself that what he saw was stunning. He told himself that he would, someday soon, wake Fran and Cindy up to witness Lazla's first light.

Later, when recounting the experience to Sagacious, he would have trouble recalling what came first. It was either the smell of burnt bodies or Garnet's howls. The sound of the crying vaegah caused Sparro to increase his speed, and their journey's remaining distance was quickly closed.

They found her on the outskirts of Quartz Mountains. Her saddle was on the verge of falling off. She was walking in a circle while shaking her head. One of her ears was missing, and droplets of blood were being flung into the air.

When they approached the injured vaegah, Dash ignored the smell and refused to let his attention wander. Sparro began shaking, and he obediently dismounted. He fixed his eyes on her. He knew, if he began looking around, if he started thinking, he would have to know. He wanted to cling to the last bit of ignorance for as long as possible.

But Sparro would have none of it. He growled and swatted Dash away from Garnet. His irritated gaze scolded the man for his weakness.

"No," Dash moaned. He tried once more to keep his attention away from the black corpses that were strewn in the distance.

Sparro headbutted Dash, and the man nearly lost his balance. As he regained his footing, his focus was lost, and he saw what remained of his hometown. The sight combined with a weakness that radiated from his hollow stomach, and he lost what remained of his strength. His shaking legs lowered him to the grass and soil, and he soon found himself staring at wispy clouds as they drifted overhead.

Chapter 22

DANE RUSHED OUT of the elevator and into his apartment on the 101st floor of Megacorp's headquarters. The sterile environment's sharp edges seemed dulled. An invisible coating of another's perspective covered his surroundings, and this caused his haste to vanish. He closed his eyes, and the fuchsia essenia in his pocket started glowing.

"Your body's temperature is unusually low, brother. It is near a dangerous level. I suggest you address it." The stilted tone of Quinsith caused Dane's eyes to open, and the luminescence in his pocket died.

"How dare you break into my apartment?" Dane hoped to see a reaction form on the face that was modeled after his own, but the unsettling smile clung to the synthetic visage.

"Father told me to find you. Our network was breached—"

"I know," Dane interrupted. This utterance came in an exasperated tone. The two words were his most used, and he was tired of them. "That's not an excuse for you to break in here."

"Father insisted that we find the terrorists as soon as possible. He is worried that their threat is valid. Their ability to infiltrate our network is a significant issue and warrants a rapid response." Quinsith strode to the center of the dimly lit room where a man-sized violet crystal sat.

Dane stared at the lifeless thing that was so much like him. The hair was the same color and style. The skin was just as pale. The face was almost identical. "And Father thinks you will be of help, how?" he asked. The red crescent of Rosa peeked at him through the open blinds as he followed the thing he called his brother.

"Prior to the breach, Site Seven's network connection was disrupted. We have no immediate data to analyze. The surveillance ring around the site is too vast to accurately and swiftly study." Quinsith smiled and exposed rows of bright white teeth. "You and your huge essenia are needed. I will assist you in tracking and analyzing whatever is revealed. When the voice of the terrorist is matched with a face, I will be able to identify her by way of the network."

The cold that coursed through him helped Dane keep his heart rate from elevating. "Fantastic," he muttered. "Shall we?"

Quinsith's unsettling smile melted to a grin. "Please proceed, brother."

Dane placed his hands on the violet crystal and closed his eyes. From within the unpolished essenia, a spark ignited and expanded. The purple glow filled the room with a heavy hue as Quinsith opened his mouth to speak in the voice of the woman who had interrupted Megacorp's digital streams.

"This message is to Megacorp from WAVE. We have commandeered your—"

"Enough!" Dane shouted. "I've got her." Sagacious Gard's voice began playing on multiple tracks within his mind. He picked one, and the others quieted. Her face emerged before his internal eye as the huge crystal projected a three-dimensional scene within the purple light.

The ghostlike image of a woman walked by Dane and Quinsith. As she moved, objects materialized around her. She reached to her left, and a bottle of liquor filled her hand. The place upon which it had rested briefly materialized before vanishing. "No thanks, Alex, sorry." Her words again came from Quinsith's synthetic mouth and synced with what the huge essenia was playing in Dane's mind.

Dane felt himself press his palms against the warm crystal. The scene that played within him trumped the incomplete one that took place behind him. When Quinsith stopped relaying the audio and started identifying Sagacious, Dane blocked out his stiff tone.

"But I'm this place's best customer!" Alex's shout rose above the noisy tavern. The mixture of forced lightheartedness and exasperation combined with the strained features of his face. "Do I have to beg?" he asked. The long-haired MERCENARY soldier stumbled off his stool and fell to his knees. The men who had been next to him chuckled in unison. "Oh, beautiful Nerva, goddess of love, do me the honor—"

A large dark-skinned man approached the drunken patron and glared down at him. "Alex, if you chase off the new girl, I'm going to ban you. I know you had something to do with Frey quitting, so don't give me that stupid look."

After a brief struggle with himself, Alex stood and stared into the dark-skinned man's eyes. "You just don't get it! Sasha and I are in love. We're vimates; we're meant to be!"

"My name is Sagacious."

Laughter came from Alex's friends. He shifted his glazed gaze from the dark-skinned man to her. "And that is an astonishing name, darling. Do me a favor, will you? Pour me another, and we'll go over names for our future children."

One of Alex's friends dismounted from his stool and clapped him on his back. "Okay, buddy, I think it's time to head back to the base."

"But Salacious and I need to finalize our wedding plans," Alex mumbled. His focus seemed to have shifted to maintaining his balance.

His other friend stood. "Stop being a shit-lord," he said. "You're already engaged, and if you don't stop hitting on maids, I'm going to tell—"

A hand gripped Dane's right shoulder, and the scene vanished along with the violet light. He spun around and endeavored to keep his warming body regulated and calm. "Were you able to identify her allies?" he asked.

"There appear to be six members of WAVE. I traced Sagacious Gard's movements over the last three years. Unfortunately, neither she nor any of the other members have a current social or professional presence on our network. There are three independent bank accounts that are associated with the members. I drained two and locked the other. The relevant information has been forwarded to Father."

Dane spoke slowly and evenly to keep his surprise under control. "Did you say there are six members of WAVE?"

"Yes, they are Sagacious Gard, Dash Black, Julie Dagger, Drio Brack, Cosmo Wells, and Cirrus Stark."

"Who is Cirrus Stark?" The question leapt out of Dane's mouth before he could stop himself.

"Cirrus Stark was born twenty-five years ago in Highwind. He is an ex-MERCENARY soldier who was a participant in Dr. Vayne's eighty-ninth vimtrial. Before Captain Dincht's death, he expelled Germ Stark for inappropriate conduct as well as mental and physical inadequacy. Cirrus is the newest member of WAVE. A conversation, during which he joins, was picked up by two electronic devices earlier today. Would you like to hear it?"

Dane's right hand reached for the fuchsia orb in his pocket as an alertness raced into him. The explosion was coming. It would shake the plate. His head snapped to his left. Mother's antique hourglass would shatter. It would crunch under his feet.

Quinsith stared at Dane. "They were able to infiltrate a reactor. How is that possible, Brother? Why were they not stopped prior to entering the reactor? Each reactor should have two sets of two MERCENARY soldiers guarding each respective site as per Father's request."

Dane released his fuchsia essenia and ran his hands through his stiff hair. His palms pressed the hard strands against his scalp as his fingers traveled to the back of his neck. The polar dream was wearing off as the rushing heat of the explosion drew nearer to the present. His skin felt as if it was being pricked by grass. He could smell smoke combined with an unidentifiable sweetness.

"He insisted on cutting the reactors' bid, remember? If he wants the best soldiers, he needs to provide MERCENARY with the best compensation. He can't just expect premium at a discount! People get what they pay for. Frankly, this was inevitable, wasn't it? I hope he's panicking up there."

A scene that involved Elena flashed across Dane's mind. It was altered. There were two individuals facing her. "There should only be one," he muttered. "Who are they? Where is Sagacious?"

"Brother, your behavior is becoming erratic, and your heart rate is accelerating to a dangerous level. I suggest you remove your essenia."

Dane rolled his reddening eyes and turned back to the huge crystal. His hands slapped against its sides, and he breathed in deeply. "Those recordings of Cirrus Stark joining WAVE, are they audio only?"

"There is no accompanying video," Quinsith responded. "Drio Brack's computer is one of the sources for the audio, and it is equipped with a lens, but it must have been covered."

"Find something with audio and video, so I don't have to search the entire fucking network." Dane closed his eyes and struggled to calm his mind.

Quinsith made a noise that sounded as if he was clearing his throat before speaking in the voice of Cirrus Stark. "You can't be serious."

The violet essenia burst with illumination as Dane connected the words to the source of their recording. Before his internal eye, he saw a thin young man standing in the center of a MERCENARY quad. Gray stone buildings intensified the bright red of the uniformed soldiers as they walked behind the waifish young man.

"The trauma to his system was too great. The fall would've killed anyone. The medics tried everything, but—"

"No!" The cry bounced off the surrounding buildings. The previously moving, talking soldiers stopped and went silent. Their attention searched for the source of the shout and settled on the duo that Dane was watching. After checking the angles presented by the available footage, he merged all four viewpoints. This created a three-dimensional perception, which allowed for the focusing and zooming of his view without a substantial loss in visual quality.

The ghoulish face of the skeletal figure caused Dane's concentration to waver, and the scene briefly warped before he yanked it back into place. The sunken eyes of the short-haired young man were alive with an unnerving electricity. His emaciated appearance resembled that of those with vim poisoning; a sure sign of Dr. Vayne's trials.

"Germ Stark, if you don't calm yourself, I will have you calmed." Captain Dincht's voice sounded loud and muffled.

The device that had picked up the audio must've been in his jacket pocket, Dane figured. He searched for and found a device on Cirrus. The audio was woven together with Captain Dincht's audio, and the dual sources allowed for the removal of most distortions.

"I didn't mean to hurt him; I can't control it." Cirrus's eyes welled with tears as bluish-white sparks reached across them.

A faint zapping noise could be heard before a screech of pain stabbed into Dane's ears.

"That's not true, is it, Germ? I spoke with Dr. Vayne. According to the doctor you can control it. He figures you channel the vim in your body like anyone else who performs mystics, and your essenia grounds your erratic power surges."

Cirrus ran a hand over his head. Several blond hairs fell to his shoulders as his now bloody eyes blinked rapidly. "It's not that simple, Captain."

"I spoke with Germ Yuff. It sounds like you and Germ Luneth were arguing prior to the incident. Is that right, Germ?"

"No, well, we were disagreeing." Cirrus shut his eyes, and red tears streaked down his face. "It's to be expected. Home-life and the assignments… I didn't… he's not… he can't be…"

"What confuses me is that he wasn't wearing his MERCE-NARY-issued specula. Why is that, Germ?"

"He lost it." Cirrus opened his eyes, and Dane cringed at the sight.

"He lost it," Captain Dincht echoed. "He lost it, like Germ Seymore lost his while the entry class was on assignment over the summer? A few days later, he went missing. At the time, I figured he knew he was about to be cut and gave up, but now I'm not so sure. With the unprofessional association between you two, coupled with you and Luneth's misguided union, the missing specula—"

"I didn't—"

Captain Dincht held up a hand, and Cirrus went silent. "Don't bother, Germ. I'm going to send in a request to HQ, and they will provide all pertinent electronic data around the entry class's summer assignment as well as anything involving Germ Luneth's death. If, in either case, malice is discovered, proper legal steps will be taken. Regardless of what is found, I cannot retain you in the entry class."

Dane yanked his hands from the violet essenia a fraction of a second before a rumbling rolled across the plate. Megacorp's headquarters swayed, and the surreal sensation made him feel as if he might lose his balance. The hourglass shattered after walking off the shelf that had displayed it. The near-omniscient Quinsith's surprise tugged at the ends of Dane's lips, and he turned to face Rosa and the flaming wreckage beneath her.

Chapter 23

SAGACIOUS WATCHED AS Cirrus and Julie headed toward the hall-way. Worry started to erode her confidence. It had been easy to plot and plan in the nights leading up to this point, but now that there was no turning back, unease poured into her. She shuddered as beads of sweat formed on her back.

Her daughter's caretaker for the evening was Mrs. Lesca, an older woman who frequented Seventh Heaven on week-nights. Most of Sagacious's patrons visited her establishment on weekends, while the rest of the week was reserved for diehard drinkers and those who enjoyed the atmosphere. Mrs. Lesca belonged to the latter group. Much of her time was spent alone as she sipped nonalcoholic beverages. She crubbed during her time at Seventh Heaven. Articles of clothing emerged from her wrinkled hands as she turned carkryle yarn into products, which she claimed to sell.

Darlene was welcome to spend time behind the drinktop on slow nights. Sagacious preferred that she stay away from the customers but once she gained the ability to talk and walk, she proved to be more extroverted than her mother expected.

Before she could be stopped, the little girl engaged the old woman in a conversation concerning her favorite subject.

Shortly after Darlene began lecturing Mrs. Lesca on how vaegahs hate water but love fish, Sagacious swooped in and apologized to the old woman. As she led the child back to her designated spot behind the drinktop, Mrs. Lesca objected. She told the young mother that the little girl wasn't bothering her. A desperation highlighted the old woman's words. From then on, Mrs. Lesca sat at the front of the tavern where she and Darlene entertained each other.

The possibility that the old woman might end up raising her daughter crossed Sagacious's mind, and her eyes became wet. Warm tears leaked onto her reddening cheeks. She pulled her dainty knuckles off her left hand and wiped the tears from her face.

"Do y'all need anything?" Hilda's question was directed at Brack and Wells.

"No, ma'am," Wells answered. The two men were focused on Brack's computer, which was now sitting open and facing away from the MERCENARY soldiers. "We should be able to fix everything from our computer, now that we're under your site's umbrella."

Dash sidled over toward Braver and scanned for the man's weapon. A metal rod rested against the desk. Within the center of its handle, secured by a thin silver strip, a green essenia orb rested. "Is that a cane?" Dash asked. A smile slipped across his face.

"*No!*" Braver exclaimed. "Don't they train MERCENARY soldiers anymore? Back in my day—"

"There he goes again," Hilda whispered to Sagacious.

Sagacious slid the metal knuckles back onto her left hand. She examined Hilda's kind face and wished that the female MERCENARY soldier wasn't so nice. It was easier to paint Megacorp as an evil force when its employees were cruel and heartless.

"I like your knuckles." Hilda gestured to Sagacious's hands. "They're pretty. You don't see many like that. They're so ladylike."

Sagacious balled her hands into fists. "Thanks," she said. The weapon warmed around her fingers and against her palms. "I give self-defense lessons to women. I know how to find the right gear."

"Wow, really? Is that your assignment?" Hilda asked.

Sagacious's attention scattered as she stumbled over her thoughts. "It's just a hobby," she admitted.

"How interesting—" Hilda began.

"It's done!" Brack announced. "We're connected." His dark eyes darted from the computer screen to Dash.

Sagacious drew in a deep breath. Her following actions came about without a governing thought. First, she felt herself bend back as her right arm fell behind her. Her entire body weight was then thrown behind a blow to Hilda's petite jaw. The shot sent the MERCENARY soldier to the floor a fraction of a second before a few of her teeth. The woman remained still as blood oozed from her gaping mouth.

Dash jabbed Braver's face. The impact was minor. As the MERCENARY soldier's head fell back, he reached for the older man's rod, but Braver recovered quickly and grabbed his weapon. He backed out of the curved desk's enclosure. "I knew something was wrong with your story," he muttered. Braver's eyes darted from terrorist to terrorist as if trying to decide which one to beat into submission first.

Dash and Sagacious started to close in on him. Before the two came within the range of Braver's rod, a loud bang reverberated throughout the lobby. A green sphere of light flashed around Braver, and a bullet clinked to the floor.

"Hmm, I guess Cirrus was telling the truth," Wells muttered. He lowered the gun and shrugged.

"You're an idiot," Braver spat. "Artillery enthusiasts are more pathetic than baby boopuffs. Did you really think—" he began.

Dash took advantage of Braver's distraction and leapt upon him. The thick sole of his tan boot sunk into the older man's stomach. The kick caused both men to lose their footing. While Dash regained his stance, Braver gasped for air and faltered in Sagacious's direction.

She reached for the rod and yanked it out of his hands. His wrinkled expression was flushed, and he bore a grimace that was amplified by his aged skin. "Give me that," he rasped.

She discarded the weapon. It flew a few meters into the lobby and clattered to the floor. Fear washed over Braver's face as he regained his composure. He backed up so that the terrorists were in front of him.

"You're not much without your cane, old man," Dash taunted. He was ready and eager to tackle the MERCENARY soldier.

Another bang resounded through the lobby. This time there was no protective green flash. The bullet from Wells's gun struck Braver in the center of his forehead, and blood sprayed as the back of his head ruptured. The bullet finished its journey in the wall behind its target and was followed by a red mist that clung to the previously pristine surface.

"Damn it!" Brack yelled. "How many times do I have to tell you? Don't fire your gun so close to my ears!"

"Useless, huh?" Wells asked. He glared at Braver's corpse.

Dash wiped specks of warm blood from his face. "Yeah, man, I appreciate the assist, but that wasn't necessary." He smirked. "Not while Sagacious is here." He examined the motionless victim of her powerful blow. "Seriously, I'm impressed. You walloped her!"

"I like to watch girls fight, but damn that was so fast," Wells added.

Sagacious stepped around the red halo that was oozing from what was left of Braver's head. "Let's do this, boys." She strode over to Brack's computer. "Lens!" she demanded.

"Yo, girl," Dash hollered. He tossed a black hood to Sagacious before grabbing another one from his purse.

Brack pressed a button on his computer, and a dark square partially ejected from one of its sides. He pulled the thin block of technology from the device and unfolded it. After a finger stroked one of the corners of its head, its face lit up with an image. "Okay, you should try to change your voice when you speak. I've got an audio filter to shift the tones, but every little bit will help." He pressed a few more of the tiny buttons on the lens with the tip of a fingernail. "I think it'd look good if we could get the empty lobby behind you."

"No, no, do it over there." Wells pointed to Braver's corpse. "So you can show the dead MERCENARY soldier."

"What are you talking about? The woman would be in the shot of the lobby!" Brack shouted.

"Boys!" Sagacious interrupted.

Chapter 24

WEISS KEFKA READIED his shotgun while his eyes stayed fixed on the humphrit. The impressive beast was standing close to a nearby pond as it chewed on trees that stretched high above the water. It tore a chunk from the green ceiling, and unobstructed light made its way into the area.

Its sight appeared, from Weiss's distant perspective, obstructed by the fine fur that pushed outward from its skin. Such a large trophy, he thought, would make this trip more worthwhile. He'd have it stuffed, shipped back home, and it would be the game room's center piece.

He flicked the safety off. The beast's large midsection found its way into the crosshairs, and he fired. As the shotgun kicked his shoulder, a bright sphere of white flashed around where he had aimed. The humphrit's relatively small head turned from side to side as it surveyed the area for the source of the noise. It paused, as it looked in Weiss's direction, before it again began tearing leaves from overhead.

Stupefied by the idea that this big animal was not only in possession of essenia but could somehow use it, he removed his hunting cap and ran a hand through his sweaty rust-red hair. "What the…" he mumbled.

Long fuzz, on one side of the humphrit, distorted in a vertical line. The woman, who dismounted, took a few seconds to adjust the white dress that covered her body before marching in his direction. He gaped at the sight. Her lengthy hair was as devoid of color as her dress, and he expected to be greeted by an elderly woman. This thought was soon forgotten, however, when her youthful features came within view.

As she neared him, she too appeared surprised. Her furious pace slowed as she closed the distance between the two. When he recognized that she noticed their tribal adjacency, he smiled and waved. This seemed to reignite her initial anger, and she hastened the last few steps.

Before he could greet her, she grabbed his weapon, yanked it out of his hands, and began marching away. Stunned, he watched as she threw his shotgun into the pond. As it splashed and sank out of sight, he blinked rapidly in disbelief. She turned around, marched back to where she had confiscated the weapon, and slapped him. The action was softened by his short beard, and he felt the urge to grin in response.

"You could've killed someone with that thing!" she shouted.

A hand went to where she had struck him. The bristly hair brushed against his fingertips, and he found himself unable to discover a proper response. He couldn't recall such treatment at any previous point in his life. Since the day he was born, everyone had always regarded him well. Whether they meant it or not was of no interest to him, but at least they pretended to respect him.

"Explain yourself!" she pressed. Her hands found her hips and her head tilted.

He took a step toward her with the intention of invading her personal space. His eyes locked on hers, and he tried his best to keep his interest in her undetectable. "That's the point of a gun." He intended for the words to come out more forcefully. To his ears, they almost sounded like a request. His face warmed. "I always shoot to kill," he finished.

"So, you wanted to shoot and kill Noah? Why? What did he do to you?" The volume of her voice carried her words to the humphrit's ears, and his otherwise constant chewing paused as he briefly looked to her.

Weiss no longer could smother his enjoyment. His tone revealed that he was on the verge of laughter. "It has a name?"

"Of course, he has a name! You have one, don't you? Why can't he have one too?" Her questions fired at him as if she was using his now waterlogged weapon.

"Weiss Kefka," he responded.

"What?" she demanded.

"My name is Weiss Kefka."

"What makes you think I care what your name is? You almost killed me and my friend." Her arms crossed as she waited for him to try and justify his actions.

"Yours?" His amusement with her anger was clearly irritating her, and he was sure to keep it in his tone and on his face.

"What?"

"Your name, what is your name?" he asked.

"It's Celeste, but I—"

His hands found one of hers before his lips kissed its back. He purposefully accentuated the sentiment and didn't pucker. The wiry hairs on his face pressed into her skin, and he suppressed a reaction to the animal's smell.

A laugh burst from her, and she yanked her hand away as she stepped back. "What in Lazla's name are you doing?"

"Where I come from, it is how a gentleman makes a lady's acquaintance." He took a step toward her. "It's proper etiquette among my people," he explained.

"Who are your people?" She rubbed where his beard had tickled her.

His eyebrows lifted, and he attempted to ascertain if she was playing with him. "The Kefkas…" He purposefully trailed off to give her time to recognize the familial name.

She shook her head. "I've never heard of the Kefkas." She smirked as he became crestfallen.

"You can't be serious. My grandfather was a chail baron who practically monopolized the industry. Our family controls Megacorp—the largest company on Pearl. Everyone knows the Kefka name."

She shook her head and basked in his frustration. "Not everyone," she teased.

His tone became skeptical. "Are you a Farron native?"

"Is that so hard to believe?"

For a moment he was unsure of what to say. It felt as if she was taunting him. For Weiss, this was a strange sensation. He was usually the one to toy with others. "Actually, yes, it is hard to believe," he admitted.

"Why is it hard to believe, Weiss Kefka?"

The way she articulated his name was either meant to be condescending or seductive. His inability to pin it vexed him. "You know, don't make me say it," he sighed.

"No, I don't know, I'm just an ignorant girl from Farron."

He rolled his eyes. "Well, you do make friends with giant fluffy—"

She stood on her toes, reached for the back of his head, and drew his face close to hers. She caressed her lips against his. His instincts kicked in, and he kissed her.

Their lips parted, and he pulled away. The soft light of the bedroom's candles made her look as if she was glowing. He wanted her to hold him all night, but he knew he could never ask. He wanted to confess his love for her, but he was almost certain it was too soon for such words. He wanted to ask her to come back to Urba with him, but what would people say? One of the most powerful men on Pearl goes to Farron and finds a new bride? Madness, he thought.

"What are you thinking?" he asked.

"I think this feels familiar," she answered.

He couldn't stop himself. He reached for her and brushed a bit of her hair back before caressing a cheek. "I know, I feel comfortable with you too."

"No, I mean, I feel the same way, but doesn't this seem familiar? It's as if I dreamed this exact moment a long time ago, and I forgot about it, but now that it is actually happening, I'm kind of remembering it."

He didn't know what she meant. Briefly, he attempted to understand, but it was like trying to hold onto water. Her skin was golden in the candlelight, and he felt himself growing aroused again. He edged toward her, and their lips met.

"Damn it, Weiss!" She pushed him away. "I'm not leaving my home. I love you, but I can't live in that place." She turned from him and cast her gaze over the terrace. Rosa was beginning to rise, and a chill shook her.

"Don't tell me you love me if you refuse to be a part of my life!" He stepped to her side and demanded her attention with his stare. "Why are you afraid of making this real?" he pressed.

As she looked to him, she began to feel as if she was in a play. Everything that was being said felt as if it had been said sometime long ago. She almost brought it up, but she was too angry with him.

"Why do I have to uproot my life for you?" she demanded.

"Celeste, I would move here for you if I could, but I need to be in Urba. I have millions of employees who depend on me. With all the changes now and in the near future, the company requires my close attention. Do you understand that? I need to go back. I have a job to do; people are waiting for me."

She didn't want to tell him, but he deserved to know. "I'm pregnant." The words were accompanied by flowing tears. Humid wind came in a gust, and she walked past him and back into her bedroom.

His mouth opened in preparation to speak, but he was too taken aback. After a few seconds, he followed her. He stared at her midsection. "Are you sure?"

"Yes, I'm very sure," she muttered.

He ran his hands over his hair. The stiff strands pressed against his scalp. He wanted to tell her that she had no choice about it now. She had to come with him to Urba. His woman and his happiness were important to him, but a child was central to his future and his legacy. She could refuse him, but she could not refuse him his offspring.

She saw his thoughts in his eyes, and she turned from him. The familiar sensation of this moment pressed into her as the emotions intensified, and she walked across her bedroom in an attempt to get away from them. Her mother's antique hourglass drew her attention, and she stared at the amber sand within it. She thought about turning it over and watching the grains flow, but she wasn't sure whether or not she was meant to tip it. She wasn't sure how to break the script or if she should.

"Celeste, be my wife. Come back to Urba with me. Bear my children. Grow old with me, and I promise to spend every day making you happy that you chose to be a part of my life."

She wanted to turn around and kiss him. It would be a dream come true if she just let it happen, but she couldn't. The white essenia, which was nestled within her hair and supported by an iridescent clasp, was broadcasting the wisdom of the fallen. Farron was safe for her and her future children. Individuals who died on the continent usually had lived simple but happy lives, while those who passed away in Urba often spoke of nothing but misery and petty woes. Her mother had raised her on Farron for that reason, and she thanked her every day for it.

Gravel weighed down his voice. "Please Celeste, I love you."

"I can't!" she screamed. "Make it stop! Please, make it stop."

The midwife caught Celeste's eyes with hers. "You can do it, girl. Everything is happening as it should. You're lucky. Many women aren't as fortunate as you. All you have to do is push. Don't tell me you can't do that. Every woman can do that."

Celeste's words exploded from her. "I hate you!"

"Yeah, join the club," the midwife responded. "Just push, girl. Breathe and push. Any woman can do it. I've seen tiny women give birth to the progeny of giants. So, don't you— some pasty girl from the mainland—tell me you can't."

Celeste used all the ire that she felt toward the old woman as fuel to push. The pain and pressure intensified for what felt like forever. Finally, she felt a baby leave her.

The midwife cut the cord and cleaned the screaming newborn. "He's got your lungs, Mom," she muttered. "Do you want to see him before he goes to Dad?"

The countless instances when she had nodded and kissed orange wispy hair had resulted in an almost unbearable sense of loss each time. If she could avoid the agony, she would. Her head shook, and she bit her tongue before her eyes slammed shut.

"There's that maternal instinct that everyone talks about," the midwife quipped. She motioned for an assistant, and the baby was taken away. "Okay girl, one more to go, just breathe and push."

Chapter 25

AT THE TIME of Reactor Seven's destruction, Quinsith was the thirty-eighth Dane replica. As time passed and the iterations came and went, the engineers were instructed to program slight differences from Dane. By Q38, as his creators called him, Quinsith's personality and decision-making skills were well tuned to Dane and his preferences.

While the destruction of Reactor Seven quaked the plate, Quinsith's software was flooded with tens of thousands of urgent notifications. The location of the destruction was immediately known, and he detected that personnel were being directed to what remained of Reactor Seven's site. As the shaking passed and the monstrous noise faded, he understood the extent of the damage. The entire reactor had been obliterated along with a radius that encompassed surrounding businesses and one Megacorp residential building.

One urgent notification subverted his routine. The angry voice of his father yelled from the top floor of Megacorp's headquarters. He had made the same deduction. Dane was responsible for allowing the attack on Reactor Seven to take place.

"Brother," Quinsith began, "I estimate that it is in our best interests to prepare a countermeasure proposal for Father before we heed his request."

Dane turned from the window with raised eyebrows. "You want to make him wait?"

Quinsith shook his head and attempted to formulate a proper response. "He is enraged at the moment. If we go up there with nothing to offer—"

Dane held up a hand. "He will take his anger with me out on you," he finished.

"He has previously done it."

Blood started dripping from Dane's nostrils. The red droplets splashed onto his white suit before he realized what was happening. When his attention was drawn to the growing mess, he tilted his head back and walked across the large room. Shards of the broken hourglass crunched beneath the soles of his shoes as he reached into a pocket and removed his glowing fuchsia orb.

With his nose awkwardly tilted toward the ceiling, he placed his essenia atop a nest of interwoven gold strips. As the distance between Dane and his crystal grew, the orb's pink light faded. Quinsith watched as his brother disappeared down a short hall and passed through an open door.

"What's it like?" Dane shouted.

"What do you mean?" Quinsith's volume and tone mimicked Dane's.

"Dying, what is dying like?" Dane emerged wearing a white t-shirt. His face was clear of blood, but his hair had lost its uniformity; a few stiff strands pointed in random directions.

"I doubt what I experience is analogous to what you will experience when you die."

Dane rolled his eyes. "Well, what do *you* go through?"

"When I know it's coming, dread overcomes me. I begin to hyperventilate. I anticipate the pain, and the mind-set tends to amplify the physical aspects. When I stop processing information, there is nothing to tell. One moment I am thinking and feeling, and then everything stops."

"You still get scared, even though you know I will bring you back?" Dane asked.

"You can't bring me back." The words slipped from Quinsith's lips. "You bring back a copy, often slightly altered, of a programming framework and memory compilation. I'm not the same as the thirty-seventh iteration, nor was he the same as the thirty-sixth. If a thirty-ninth already existed, I wouldn't know. Only I am me."

A grimace passed over Dane's face before he responded. "Let's think of a plan then. Father will want to crush WAVE as soon as possible. Not only for the revenge but also to keep the public's confidence from waning. We could offer to capture and execute WAVE; we could broadcast it live over the network."

"That won't be enough," Quinsith responded. "Father would expect nothing less than that. The cost of Reactor Seven's destruction will be gargantuan. Rebuilding it is only a fraction of the calculation. The topside inhabitants of Division Seven will expect financial restitution. The reactors are the economic hubs of the divisions. The impacted people will pressure the government to demand recompense. All grievances, real and imagined, may be seen as reason enough. The variables and possibilities are so numerous that I cannot accurately project how much Megacorp will have to pay. It's possible that the company's continued existence is in jeopardy."

"That's ridiculous, Quinsith."

"The public's aggravation might feed on itself if the topside Division Seven residents aren't satisfied. A political and economic revolution is possible. The people could demand action. If the government refuses, they might choose to overthrow the current paradigm. The ensuing chaos could result in a public confiscation of Megacorp's assets. The corporation would be shattered."

Dane returned to the window and stared at the smoldering wreckage in the distance. The orange flames were hypnotic as they whipped into the ever-present wind. Blue lights were rushing toward the scene from the heart of the division as well as from Division Six and Division Eight.

"So, the problem isn't just WAVE but all of Division Seven," Dane mumbled. An idea crept into him as connections were made within his mind. "And what if WAVE had been more ambitious? What if they had gone after Division Seven's support pillar? If the entire division was in ruins, things would be much simpler, wouldn't they?"

"WAVE's cited goal is to protect Pearl." Quinsith joined his brother at the window and followed his gaze. "Their target was the reactor because they believe the utilization of vim for commercial purposes harms the planet. Regardless, they wouldn't have attempted such a plan on Division Seven. Their homes and families are, for the most part, located in the slums of Division Seven. If the pillar fell, it would destroy much of what they hold dear."

Dane smiled. "It's perfect!" he exclaimed. "That's what we will present to Father as a solution. The clandestines will be able to pull it off."

"I don't understand," Quinsith admitted. Annoyance nagged at him, and the discomfort caused him to check his physical state. When nothing was found out of order, he sent a report to the engineers responsible for his creation and maintenance.

"The pillar, brother, *the pillar*!" Dane turned to Quinsith and began dancing in place. His feet tapped a crude mimic of a jig from I Want to be Your Lovebird.

"I still don't—"

Dane's feet stopped moving and he grabbed one of Quinsith's hands before bringing it to his chin. "Quinsith Kefka, this is your brother, Dane Kefka. Can you hear me? Can you recognize the vibrations—"

"You're mocking me again, aren't you?"

"I wouldn't have to if you weren't so slow."

Quinsith pulled his hand from Dane's face. "I'm not slow. I process information at the speed of light. If someone compared us, you would be considered many times slower."

"You say that, but I seem to recall having to explain things to you many times over the decades."

"Quit making fun of me, and tell me why you are so excited."

"We will have the clandestines bring down Division Seven's support pillar, thereby literally crushing WAVE and everyone they know and love. I'll have them make it appear as if WAVE did it, so the public's rage will focus on an enemy of Megacorp. Not only will it satiate Father's desire for revenge, but it should also solve a lot of the other problems. It's a simple solution to a complicated problem, and you know how he's fond of such concepts."

Numbers, possibilities, and sure outcomes ran through Quinsith's mind as he considered Dane's words. His brother was right. If they successfully executed such a plan, it would result in a satisfactory outcome for Megacorp and the Kefkas. It was their best available option, and if they framed it properly, they might be able to dissuade their father from violence. With the possibility of his death dwindling in probability, Quinsith nodded. As he did so, guilt nagged at him. He forwarded another report after not detecting any physical issues.

Chapter 26

CIRRUS AND JULIE jogged into the lobby as the rest of WAVE wrapped up their broadcast. His pace slowed when he noticed Hilda's body. Blood dribbled from her mouth onto the otherwise immaculate floor.

Sagacious turned toward the new arrivals and removed her hood. She flashed Cirrus a smile. "Well?" she prodded.

"I set the bomb for thirty minutes a few minutes ago," Julie reported.

Cirrus bent down and checked Hilda's pulse. She was still alive. He rolled her onto her back and examined her. The green orb and its ornate setting remained in place. "Good," he mumbled.

"A few minutes?" Sagacious pressed. She tossed her hood to Dash.

Julie glanced at her timepiece. "It was set six minutes and thirty-six seconds ago," she specified.

Sagacious nodded, and she slapped her hands together. Her metal knuckles clanked as they bounced off each other. "Our broadcast interrupted every streaming program on Megacorp's network. They know we're in one of Urba's reactors, but I didn't say which one. Hopefully, that will buy us some extra time.

"We'll meet back at headquarters. If you're not back by Lazla's first light, the worst will be assumed. Remember, be smart, and take scenic routes." Sagacious's rushed tone was nervous, and her fidgeting added to her projected state of mind. She seemed to not know what to do with her hands. They fumbled over each other, to her sides, and finally to her hips, where her bare fingers drummed against the waistband of her short pants.

Dash looked from his purse to Cirrus. "Yeah, and if you're caught, keep your fucking mouth shut," he interjected. After his focus returned to organizing the contents of the bag, his smile returned.

"Since this was my idea, and let's face it, if there is a leader here, it's me. I'll be the last one to leave," Sagacious said. "Who wants to go first? Cirrus?"

Cirrus's attention broke from surveying the scene. The corpse of Braver appeared to have no essenia on it, and he momentarily assumed one of the others had taken it, but then his gaze fell upon the rod and its green orb. "No," he answered. "You should go first. You have a daughter."

"Yeah, Sagacious," Brack concurred. "He's right. If anyone should have the best shot at getting out of this intact, it's you."

"Fine, whatever, I tried; there's no time to debate this. My conscience is clear." She jaunted toward the front of the lobby as she continued to speak to the others. "Not a word to anyone. No names, no locations, don't talk to anyone." She pushed open a glass door. "Good luck," she called back.

"I like it when she's bossy," Wells grunted.

"Whatever, man." Brack folded up his computer and jogged toward the glass doors. He watched her disappear in one direction and decided on his own as he left the group.

"Thanks for the help, Cirrus," Wells said. "I'm sorry I treated you like vaegah shit. If we get a big blast out of this, it'll be thanks to you." He reached out and grabbed one of the ex-MERCENARY soldier's hands. "Did you see that, Dash? That's called class. Someone in this group should have it. Okay, whatever, bye everyone!" He jogged to the front of the lobby, hesitated, and then left the group.

"What happened?" Cirrus asked. He gestured to Braver's body.

"The dumb shit was protected by a will field, but he kept his essenia in his weapon," Dash said. "Sagacious was able to wrestle it from him, and Wells popped him."

Cirrus nodded. Hilda and Braver's ineptitude had been shocking, but by this time, Dash's explanation made sense. He waited a couple of seconds for the next member of WAVE to exit the scene. "Well, who's next?" he prodded.

Dash pointed to Hilda. "You checked her pulse, right? Is she alive?"

"Barely," Cirrus admitted.

Dash moved toward the unconscious woman. "I'll finish her," he growled.

"I doubt that's necessary, the explosion will do it," Cirrus responded.

Dash gave Cirrus a confused look. "What about the will field thing? Won't that, like, protect her or something?"

Cirrus felt his face flush. "Right, you're right, if she has a bond with it, it will block the flames as well as anything that might otherwise fall on her, but with the smoke, and—"

"By all holy light, I get it," Dash interrupted. "I don't need a tutorial right now." He bent toward her and covered her nose and mouth. He stared up at Cirrus. "We need to make sure she is dead." His expression became a grimace as he tightened his grip over Hilda's bloody face.

The thin body briefly convulsed beneath his grip. When she was still, he withdrew his red hand and wiped the warm ooze onto her MERCENARY jacket. As he did so, Cirrus glared from him to her essenia pendant. Dash's eyes crawled over the body as he comprehended his actions. He stood up and trotted out of the building without another word.

Julie walked over to the rod that Sagacious had discarded and picked it up. "His essenia is still in this."

Cirrus pulled his eyes from the broken woman. "Give it to me," he demanded.

She hesitated.

He stomped over to her and snatched it before gesturing toward the glass doors. "You better go," he insisted. "I'll see you back at headquarters."

She stared at him for a moment. Unease framed her features. "Stay safe," she mumbled. The heavy door slammed behind her.

Wind rushed to greet her and yanked her breath into the cool air. Her unruly hair broke free of its red strip of fabric, and brown strands flew in countless directions. The material fluttered into the invisible ocean of air and surfed high before diving down and away from the front of the reactor.

Elena beckoned her long whip to her side with a tug, and it slipped off the backseat of the vehicle. After the door was shut, the driverless chocorod sped away. She stared in disbelief at the blue taillights. "How does he expect me to get back?" she wondered aloud.

As she turned to face the reactor, she noticed a red strip of fabric flying not far from her. She reached out and snatched it from the air. She briefly examined it before returning it to the dark sky with a flick of a wrist.

The sight of Julie struggling to shove her hair into the back of her shirt caused Elena's eyebrows to lift. She hadn't expected to so easily come across the terrorist. While on her way, she had mentally prepared herself for the confrontation that was promised to take place and had concluded that anyone deft enough to overcome the reactor's security would be elusive and formidable.

A crack split through the gushing wind as Elena elevated an arm and yanked it down. The terrorist's attention shifted from attempting to manage her hair to the woman dressed in MERCENARY red. Despite the surplus of air around her, Julie struggled to catch her breath.

Elena recognized dawning fear rise from within the terrorist and cracked her whip again in an attempt to stoke the emotion. She detected no apparent weapon or accessory on the young woman; a sign that those who had assisted her in infiltrating the reactor and broadcasting her message couldn't be far.

"Where are the others?" Elena demanded.

Julie's mouth opened and closed. A hand swiped at the readying tears that were forming.

Elena adjusted her grip on her weapon and glared at her target. "Speak up!" Her sharp words dulled as they traveled to Julie's ears.

"T-They're gone." Julie's voice struggled to get over the relentless wind.

Elena's focus faltered as she recalled Dane's words. Questions darted around her mind before she could beat them back. He seemed to know the content of the terrorist's message as it was being delivered. How did he know where to send her? How did he know there would only be one terrorist left when she arrived?

Julie's body started to tremor, and she hugged herself in an attempt to stop the involuntary movement.

One of the crystal orbs at Elena's waist came alive with green light. As she focused on the rushing air around the young woman, it briefly stilled. "Where did they go? Tell me, and I won't send you to Rosa."

Despite the warmth that was regenerating within her, Julie couldn't stop shivering. She didn't want to die. While she had known it was a possibility, she had convinced herself that no matter how WAVE's plans turned out, she would be protected by the righteousness of her actions. She was fighting for the planet. Surely, she had assumed, such a force for good would be shielded from harm.

Chapter 27

CELESTE WAS LOST. She looked around at the dozens of people who were walking by her. There were so many of them. It was as if they were blood cells in a human body. They flowed in every direction in an organized rush. She was afraid to move. She was afraid to disrupt the delicate system with her presence.

Grace squeezed a hand, and the mother looked to her daughter. The girl's young face revealed as much terror as she was trying to conceal. Celeste forced a smile and hoped that it was comforting. "Isn't this fun?" she asked.

"No," Grace answered. "I want to go home."

"I know, I want to go home too, but we have a job to do."

Celeste inhaled and dove into the moving crowd of people. Her daughter stayed close to her side as she moved through the bodies. The countless voices around her combined with the confused terror that the white essenia was delivering into her mind. She was grateful every time she managed to brush up against one of the strangers around her. The brief moments of contact managed to push out excess noises, and she was able to focus.

When she and Grace first arrived in Urba, she tried to reassure those who were flowing to the reactors, but it was no use. They were too frightened. Their near-constant screaming was almost unbearable, and she wanted to yank the white essenia from its place within her hair and toss it from the plate.

As a woman in a red uniform walked by the mother and daughter, she bumped in to Celeste. The cacophony of voices within her mind briefly dwindled to one, and she listened. While the moment of clarity quickly passed, hope sprung up within her.

With no better idea of how to get the woman's attention, Celeste shouted her name. "Priscilla!"

The woman stopped and turned around. She looked from Grace to Celeste. They crossed the short distance, and the relief in the mother's eyes kept Priscilla's attention. "I'm sorry, do I know you?" she asked.

"We need to speak with Weiss." The words escaped Celeste in a rush. She was afraid that the information she had just received would soon be lost in the sea of confusion and terror that threatened to drown her mind.

Priscilla's head tilted. "What?" she asked.

"As soon as possible, we need to speak with Weiss Kefka. You're still part of his security detail, right?"

"Uh, right, but I don't—"

"Your mother is so proud of you," Celeste interjected. "She doesn't want you to worry about your father. He's not a burden for you to bear. She's sure he will be fine without her. You don't have to—"

"Who are you?" Confusion and shock mingled in Priscilla's tone. "My mother is dead."

"Yes, I know. It was recent. A few days ago, her heart stopped while she slept. Your father cried for hours before he could bring himself to tell anyone. She was afraid you'd find out from someone else because you were one of the last people he told."

Priscilla's eyes became coated in glass. Her gaze was frozen on Celeste. "How can you know that?" she demanded.

"She spoke to me, I can hear her and all of the others. They're terrified. They need your help. Your mother needs your help. Please, take me to Weiss, so we can stop this madness before it's too late."

"What? I don't—"

"The reactors!" Celeste screamed.

Grace gravitated closer to her mother as she noticed the people around them looking their way. "I want to go home," she whispered. "Please, mommy."

Some of Celeste's hair had freed itself from its clasp, and the constant wind pulled it into the air. She attempted to push it down as she realized how it must be adding to the unfortunate image that she was projecting. "The reactors," she began again, "they are devouring the dead. Your mother is in danger of being consumed by one of them. Everything you loved about her, the memories that made her an individual, all of it will be burned up in a reactor if you don't help us get to Weiss right now."

Priscilla gulped as the terrifying words combined with her knowledge of the holy texts. She had dismissed the stories as the energy revolution improved her life. But as she stared into the stranger's eyes and listened to her words, she found it impossible to dismiss what was being said. Even if the possibility was slight, the idea that her mother's afterlife could be ended, the idea that she was still somewhere but in jeopardy, kept Priscilla where she stood.

"Please, Weiss and I know each other. If you just tell him I'm here, he will want to see me. He will listen to me, I know it. We can save your mother and everyone else, but we have to hurry."

Priscilla looked away and wiped her eyes. She paused. "Come with me, and I'll get you into Megacorp's headquarters and near his office, but I can't guarantee he will meet with you."

They traveled on foot from the District One train station to the center of the plate where the tallest skyscraper on Pearl pierced the gray blanket that covered the day. The mother and daughter closely mimicked and followed Priscilla as she navigated them through the maze of electronic walkways. The distance that they traveled would've taken at least a day to walk if not for the technological shortcuts. As they zipped over the surface of the plate, occasionally they were carried into the sky, above roads that were packed with vehicles.

When they arrived at Megacorp's headquarters, both mother and daughter stared at the opulence that surrounded the building. Massive statues of men and women supported the stone entrance of the glass and steel edifice. Fountains of liquid silver and gold spurted their respective metals beneath transparent barriers. Plant-life lined the building, and Grace marveled at the collection of colors.

Priscilla led the mother and daughter by dozens of stone steps that led to the entrance. She stopped at a barely visible door on one side of the steps. As she approached the entrance, a blue light swept over her. "Priscilla Junyn and two guests." Her words caused the door to retract and slide to one side.

Behind the entrance, a sea of red greeted them. It seemed, to Celeste, everyone was dressed in the same jacket and pants as Priscilla. Grace briefly locked eyes with a man and smiled at him.

"This way," Priscilla murmured. "We'll take the kitchen's elevator to minimize our obstacles."

They pushed through two swinging doors, and the red uniforms became white. The aroma of freshly baked bread morphed into the smell of cooking meat. A sizzling noise cut through the air while they turned a corner. Priscilla pressed a button to call the kitchen's elevator and winked at Grace as they came to a brief stop.

"I'm hungry," Grace said.

Celeste readjusted her sweaty grip on her daughter and forced a positive tone. "We'll get something to eat soon, okay?"

"Okay," Grace mumbled.

"She's adorable," Priscilla whispered.

They stepped into the elevator, and the guests' escort pressed the button for the 100th floor. Another blue light swept over Priscilla before the elevator sped upward. The ascent, having been both Celeste and Grace's first elevator ride, caused them to lean against the back wall as their eyes explored the rising box.

David L Van Horne

"Can you hear my mother now?" Priscilla asked.

Celeste's free hand reached out, and Priscilla hesitantly met it with one of her own. The chattering crowd in Celeste's mind quieted. "Yes, she wants you to tell your father that the key to the safe is behind the portrait that hangs above their fireplace."

Priscilla wiped away tears. "You can really hear her, can't you?" she asked.

"When someone close to us dies, our vim remains connected to them. You may not be able to see her or hear her, but she is still a part of you, and you are still part of her."

Words bubbled up beneath now pouring tears. "Will you tell her that I love her?" Priscilla asked.

"She knows. She will be with you until the end," Celeste explained. The elevator doors pulled apart, and Celeste released Priscilla's hand.

"This is as far as I can get you." Priscilla cleared her throat and sniffled. "Have his secretary tell him you are here, and hopefully he'll make time for you. Either way, when you leave, go to the lobby and walk straight to the exit to best avoid potential problems."

"Thank you, Priscilla." Celeste embraced her. "Your mother loves you too."

More wetness began trickling down Priscilla's cheeks as the elevator doors closed behind the mother and daughter.

Grace admired the clean beauty of the 100th level's lobby. The bright white of the ceiling and walls coupled with the white marble of the floor to create the illusion that they were walking into a cloud. "Mommy, it's so pretty," she whispered.

"Yes, it is, Grace." Her hushed tone mirrored her daughter's.

As they approached the semicircle desk that held an attractive woman, the secretary followed protocol and stood to greet them. "Hello ma'am, may I get your name and the scheduled time for your appointment with Mr. Kefka?"

"Hello," Celeste responded. She attempted to mirror the secretary's cordiality. "My name is Celeste, and this is Grace. We don't have an appointment, but I'm sure if you tell him we are here, he will want to see us."

The secretary's eyes grew wide. "You don't have an appointment? Well, you need an appointment to see Mr. Kefka. May I see your guest pass?"

"My what?" Celeste asked.

"How did you get up here without a guest pass?" The secretary picked up an electronic device from her desk and began furiously tapping on it.

"Please, if you just tell him Celeste and Grace are here, he will want to see us."

As the two women spoke, Grace released her mother's hand and walked past the semicircle desk. The cloud around her surely contained Fates, she thought. She wanted to meet the one responsible for flowers and ask him why there were no yellow ones.

After turning a corner and walking a bit more, she passed in front of a glass wall. Two men stood beyond the barrier. They appeared to be talking and laughing. The fat bald man appeared to be illustrating a point by making flagrant gestures. The man with the red hair and beard was hunched over as he reacted to the other.

It took Weiss a few seconds to notice the miniature version of Celeste, but when he did, his laughter dropped from his chest like a stone. His face went from rosy to pale in an instant. Paul noticed the changing atmosphere and followed his gaze.

Grace waved to the two, and Paul waved back. "Is that your next appointment?" he asked. A laugh was forced in an attempt to rekindle the previous mood.

Celeste rushed to the little girl and was followed by his secretary and two MERCENARY soldiers. Dumbstruck, by the sight of his daughter and the woman he would forever consider the love of his life, Weiss had trouble understanding what he was seeing. As one of the MERCENARY soldiers pulled a small chain from his pocket and grabbed Celeste's wrists, she locked eyes with the man she would forever consider the love of her life. "Weiss!" she yelled.

Although the glass wall that separated them muffled her use of his name, it was enough to yank him back to coherence. He rushed from his office and to her. As his secretary and the MERCENARY soldiers began babbling their apologies, he reached for her and brushed a bit of her hair back before caressing a cheek.

Chapter 28

THE YELLOW EYES of Darkness greeted Dane and Quinsith as they stepped into their father's apartment on the top level of Megacorp's headquarters. The black vaegah's vertical pupils narrowed to slits while she uncurled herself and rose from her position on the marble floor. A low growl of recognition escaped the gigantic cat's closed mouth. She turned from the two and began sashaying out of the foyer. As the pads of her feet pressed against the polished marble, the tips of her bladelike claws clicked in a steady pace that echoed throughout the cavernous room.

Darkness's tail wormed in the air as if an independent entity. The extremity pointed to Dane and Quinsith before swinging to one side and wrapping around a man-sized doll. The vaegah passed beneath an archway, while her tail waved the doll in front of the pseudo brothers.

"Why is she doing that?" Dane whispered.

"She wants us to follow her," Quinsith responded in a mimicked tone.

As Darkness led the two around a corner, one of the stuffed arms of the doll flew off the body and thumped against a gray wall. Her large head turned as her ears flattened. Another growl emitted from her thick neck and pushed out of her closed mouth.

"Stop it, Darkness," Dane said. "You don't have to wave that thing in our faces for us to follow you. We aren't kittens. We aren't going to wander off."

The doll moved closer to Dane, and it danced. An unseen bell jingled. The smell of it triggered his gag reflex, and he batted it away. Satisfaction filled Darkness's narrow face, and she began moving again. The doll returned to its place in front of the two.

"My racing vaegahs are just as haughty as this one," Dane said. The doll gravitated toward him again, and he smacked it back. "Every time I go to the Silver Circlet and visit the stables, I feel like they think I'm a simpleton. Once, when I asked a jockey what a slop run was, the vaegah that he was brushing gave me a condescending look. Another time, years ago, I brought a date down to the stables. I wanted to show off my prize-winning vaegahs. Well, when I tried to put a saddle on one of them, it pushed me over! It head-butted me, and I fell into the mud. I started yelling, my date started laughing, and the fucking cat, I swear to Lazla, smiled."

"It couldn't have smiled," Quinsith interjected. "Vaegahs don't have the facial muscles that are required to smile. People often project what they want to know and see onto others as well as animals."

"I know what I saw, it *smiled* at me. I'm surprised it didn't start laughing along with my date."

"If it's any consolation, vaegahs are very intelligent. Studies have shown their mental processing near or at the level of men. However, that doesn't mean they think like men. Their brain structure is much different."

"Thanks, professor," Dane quipped.

Darkness sauntered through an open doorway, and the two followed. Her tail tossed the doll to one side, and it thudded to the floor. A purr emerged and filled their father's sprawling office with the entrancing noise. She strolled toward the back of the immense room where Weiss's desk sat. From a distance, it appeared as if it was made of gold, but upon closer inspection one would've noticed the imperfections that come with wood.

Weiss shifted his focus from an electronic display on his desk to a drawer on his right side. He pulled out a fish-shaped object and waved it for Darkness to see. The purring turned into a desperate howl before Weiss tossed the fake fish to the vaegah. She caught it in her mouth and slinked to a midnight blue pillow where she collapsed. Her greedy eyes darted to Dane and Quinsith to make sure that they were not interested in her new treasure.

Weiss stood, and the brown leather chair was pushed back toward the towering window that overlooked a vertically distant metropolis. Haze caused the red glow of Rosa to spread over the scene. The well-built man's hair and full beard smoldered in the cosmic light. His brown eyes flicked from the typically dressed Quinsith to his son's choice of apparel. Dane's casual appearance added to the fury that was being suppressed beneath the aged muscle of his chest.

"Father, you will be glad to hear—" Quinsith began.

"Please don't tell me you wore *that* to your little birthday celebration." Weiss's words boomed.

Dane glanced down at the t-shirt before locking eyes with his father. "So, you remembered, but you chose not to come?"

Weiss held up a hand as if signaling Dane to stop. "Don't pretend like you wanted me to make an appearance. We both know otherwise."

"Still, an acknowledgment, sometime throughout the day, would have been fatherly of you. Honestly, I thought you had forgotten. It didn't bother me. But now that I know you remembered and still didn't say anything, wow."

"Of course, I remembered the day," he grumbled. "It's the day my life changed for the worse."

Dane's mouth dropped, and he turned to Quinsith. "He's unbelievable!"

Quinsith started to speak again, but Weiss's voice overwhelmed his words. "I'm unbelievable!" he roared. "You are the one whose actions are beyond the realm of sanity and understanding. Either through blind incompetence or fevered malice, you and your MERCENARY soldiers are responsible for *that*." He pointed to the wreckage of Reactor Seven. The thin clouds detracted from the impact of the statement.

"You're the one who cut the reactors' bid! You can't expect excellent security if you refuse to properly bid on my soldiers. Other people are willing to bid on them, and if they have the shill, they will get them."

Weiss's palms covered his beard as he inhaled deeply and endeavored to not lose control. "You are the most short-sighted person to have ever drawn breath." His hands flew from his face; his eyes were wide with frustration. "Megacorp makes a majority of its revenue from our reactors! If MERCENARY must take a financial hit, in order to maintain their security, MERCENARY must take that hit."

"So, you expect me to maintain order and the status quo with less? That's not possible."

Laughter exploded from Weiss. He bent over and the hoarse outburst continued for longer than any of them expected. Even Darkness tilted her head in surprise.

After the laughter died, and Weiss straightened himself, silence briefly filled the room. Recognizing this as an opportunity to perhaps save himself, Quinsith began speaking again. "Father, you will be glad to hear—"

"Are you going mad, Dane?"

Dane rolled his eyes and sighed. "No, Father."

One of Weiss's hands returned to his beard. "If you were going mad, it would explain what I learned from Verdel Xing this afternoon."

Dane's pale face lost what little color it had. "What?" he croaked.

"You've been utilizing my resources to chase myths for nearly half a year. clandestines, every second of every day, for half a year! When I found out, I almost couldn't believe it, but when I learned why you're doing it?" He shook his head and attempted to keep his tone from cracking. "Do you have any idea how expensive their time is?"

"Father, now that you have brought up—"

"Not now, Quinsith. I'm trying to teach my son a lesson. Dane, assigning a clandestine to stalk some girl from the slums is not only insane but a colossal waste of shill."

"No, it's not. I'm certain that she is a Sentinel—probably the last one. The information that has been gathered on her is irrefutable. She hears voices from the vimstream. She can harness it! The Promised Land will be ours if we just get her to—"

"A clandestine has witnessed her harnessing the vimstream?" Weiss asked.

Dane paused. "Well, not exactly. She has a garden in the slums. She can grow things in that soil. It's the only explanation."

"Just to be clear, you're telling me a slum girl hears voices and grows plants, and you think this is proof of a myth that involves controlling the vimstream. Do I have that right? Oh, and what, you think she will light the way to the Promised Land as predicted in the holy texts?"

"Yes," Dane replied.

Weiss's hands dropped to the golden wood of his desk, and he hunched over it. "I tried my best with you, Dane. I did everything right, and when that didn't work..." He glanced at Quinsith as he trailed off. "I did what I thought was necessary to create a man who would be a sufficient replacement for me; someone who could carry on our family's legacy." His breath escaped him, and the imposing man sank in on himself. He picked up a key from his desk and unlocked a drawer.

"Here we go again about your precious legacy. I'm sorry I won't be giving you grandkids, okay? If passing on your genes was so important, you should've had more than one child. Maybe if you hadn't married that old—"

Weiss pulled a black pistol from out of sight and pointed it at Dane's chest. "I wanted more than anything to fix you. Not just for me, but for your mother." The tears that rolled down his flushed face were the first Dane had ever seen come from his father's eyes. "But you've gone too far this time. The catastrophes that would befall this world if I let your recklessness continue, I don't want to know."

From her pillow, Darkness watched the scene unfold. It was not until her master grabbed his weapon that her snack was abandoned. Her cat eyes shifted from yellow to a green that glowed, and her pupils changed from slits to holes. The vaegah's body stood and strolled toward the confrontation. Quinsith was the first to recognize the oddity, but any reaction that he might've had was buried by what was playing out.

When Darkness was between father and son, a black fog poured from her face. The shadow consolidated as the green light, which had briefly been the vaegah's eyes, drifted to the face of the man who was growing from the shadow. As he developed, all three Kefkas recognized him.

"By all holy light," gasped Weiss. His shaking hand dropped the gun, and it clunked off the desk and onto the floor.

Aggeroth pulled his thin sword from its place on his back and shoved it into Weiss's chest. He pushed until the man's muscles touched the hilt of his sword. With awe-inspiring strength, he lifted Weiss from his feet and swung him over the desk to where Dane and Quinsith stood. By simply shifting the position of his wrist, he allowed the dying man to slip from his sword and to their feet.

"If either of you would like to excise your daddy issues, now is the time." Aggeroth's voice dripped with amusement.

Dane and Quinsith exchanged shocked glances before Quinsith dove down. He covered Weiss's gaping mouth. "Look at me, Father!" he snarled. "In my eyes! Look in my eyes!"

Weiss granted Quinsith's wish and stared into him. Blood began to bubble up the dying man's throat, and it splashed against the hand that preempted any gurgling.

"Thirty-seven times," Quinsith seethed. "You did this to me thirty-seven times. You never apologized, not once! I was created from him, and you knew it. But you didn't care. You used me over and over again to teach lessons that fell on deaf ears, and when you failed, you used me as an outlet for your rage. You aren't better than him. You are him, and if there's any justice in this universe, everything that makes you who you are will burn in one of your damn reactors."

Aggeroth stepped toward Dane and whispered into his ear. "There's something I'd like to discuss with you."

Dane tore his attention from the scene that was playing out near his feet. When he recognized the silver hair and black robe again, he felt the same shock he had experienced just a moment prior. "Y-you're dead," he gasped.

"Death and time are strange things, my friend. They aren't what they seem if you are able to understand them."

"What?"

Aggeroth waved off the question. "You and I have interests that align, and I propose that we support each other."

"I-I don't understand," Dane sputtered. He felt strange. Everything that he perceived was different but the same from before the dead man had appeared. He felt disoriented and giddy. Worry breathed down his neck while thrill danced up his spine.

"You were supposed to die. You didn't. You're acclimating as we all are. Expect to feel out of place, and gird yourself for some shockwaves. Aberrations in the fabric tend to create and suffer them."

"What?" Dane repeated.

"I'm going to need you to focus. I want you to pay attention."

The glowing green of Aggeroth's eyes provided comfort. Dane felt his pulse slow as his body relaxed. "I understand," he mumbled.

"The woman whom you seek, the one with the white hair; I think you are right. I believe she is a Sentinel."

"Plans are in motion to capture her and verify her abilities," Dane heard himself admit.

"Yes, it's why I saved you from a bullet to the chest." He poked Dane where the bullet was supposed to have gone. "I would go after her myself, but alas what she can do could just as much harm me as help me."

Dane's attention fell down to where Aggeroth had poked him, and he saw a bloody gunshot wound. He blinked, and the shirt was unscathed.

"NO!" Quinsith shouted. His blood-covered hands gripped the shoulders of Weiss's corpse. "We aren't done, Father! You need to feel this!"

Aggeroth's attention shifted to the dead body. An iridescent shimmer that only he could see was drifting in the air near

Weiss's face. The man with the glowing eyes crouched beside the corpse. His thin lips parted, and a bottomless emptiness drew the light into him.

While Dane tried to understand what he had been told, while Quinsith cursed the corpse of the closest thing he would ever have to a father, while Aggeroth devoured everything that had made Weiss Kefka an individual, Darkness was hooking one of her claws into the handle of the drawer that contained her fish snacks.

Chapter 29

CIRRUS EXAMINED THE dead man's weapon. Braver's essenia was fixed in the fist-sized handle by a thin metal strip. He ran fingers along the shaft of the smooth rod in an attempt to find a button or a switch.

His fingers passed over a line of free space near the weapon's base. He twisted both ends in opposite directions, and the silver strip retracted into the handle. The orb popped out of its setting, and he caught the crystal before it could drop and shatter. He shoved it into a jacket pocket as the rod clattered to the floor and rolled away.

There was no pause in his actions. He strode to Hilda's body and bent down toward it. First, he tried to remove her essenia pendant with one hand, but when he failed to manipulate whatever mechanism was keeping it to her chest, he used both hands. Still, however, the pendant refused to budge.

The stress that he felt amplified as the infuriating sparks over his scalp and under his arms stung at his skin. A frustrated cry escaped his lips, and he released the pendant. He was about to force the essenia out of its setting with an earthen and air combination mystic, but he stopped himself when her specula ring grabbed his attention. He let out a short laugh and retrieved the band before dropping it next to the dead man's orb.

One of his hands hovered over the pendant, and he concentrated on the strings of metal that held the round crystal in place. The silver strands grew a bright orange and slowly pulled from the green orb. He snatched it up and bit his bottom lip as he burned the tip of a finger. The treasure found its place next to the other as he walked back to Braver's corpse and swooped down to grab his specula ring.

As he gripped the handle of a glass door, he saw that Julie was standing a few meters in front of him. Her back was to the lobby, but a mixture of frustration and alarm still dragged at the black weight that clung to him. Electric pops crackled within his ears, and he clamped his hands over them to smother the energy. The pain quickly subsided, and he exited the reactor.

"You lied!" Shrill words cut through the gusting winds.

Julie's eyes broke from the direction of the voice and met Cirrus's. "I'm sorry," she mouthed.

He shook his head and stepped forward. "Get behind me," he told her.

The challenger became more visible as Cirrus passed Julie. The female MERCENARY soldier's uniform clung to her tall and shapely body. At her side, she held the handle of a thick whip that spilled onto the plate's surface. The black braid of her weapon mirrored her lengthy hair, which was tied back and restrained by the style. Beneath the beauty of her dark eyes, the thorns of a scowl warned away his appreciation for her aesthetics.

"How dare you impersonate a MERCENARY soldier?" Elena's shout burned a hole in the nonstop wind around them. She cracked her whip. "I'll break your neck for such nerve!"

"Let her go," Cirrus yelled. He attempted to keep his tone steady as his eyes fell upon Elena's yellow essenia. It rested within her belt's buckle next to a green orb. Both were alive with pulsing light. He pulled his sword from its resting place over his back.

"You're in no position to give orders!" she roared. In a fading streak of yellow, she sped at the terrorists and leapt over them. The thick body of her whip wrapped around Julie's neck in a flash.

"She's not a threat to you," he reasoned. "Let her go, and try your best with me. Come on—someone with all those medallions must have a sense of honor, right?"

Elena looked to Julie's strained face. "How gallant!" she exclaimed. "If it weren't for that awful hair, I might mistake him for a gentleman." Her actions paused. "I'm a sucker for good manners." She loosened the whip's grip, and Julie's hands rushed to her throat. "To be honest, I have orders; I'm going to have to kill you, but if he insists on going first…"

Cirrus bent toward Julie. "Are you okay?" he asked.

Julie's bloodshot eyes crept up and met his stare. She attempted to respond but failed.

Elena grinned as a realization came to mind. "I'm being irrational though, aren't I? I'm told to come here and eliminate her, but a chivalrous hero comes out of nowhere to try and stop me. It's not that I think you'll be much of a problem, but your weakness is showing, and I am a pragmatist," she concluded.

Elena held her free hand above Julie. An orange spark ignited from her palm. The fire grew to a rolling ball of flames. "Would I be wrong to assume this will handicap you for our epic final battle?" Her offensive glare drilled into him. "Say good-bye, hero."

"No!" Cirrus shouted. One hand released his sword's handle, and he pointed all four fingers at the sphere of fire. Her specula ring blinked a faint blue, and the icy mystic exploded between them. Vapor drifted from their noses and mouths before the racing winds carried away the cold.

The bright ball of heat dropped onto the back of Julie's neck. Flames raced from the point of impact and rapidly engulfed her. A shriek of pain turned to a whimper. As her body blackened, she went quiet, and what remained of the young woman collapsed.

"Coward!" Cirrus bellowed. Both hands tightened around the handle of his heavy blade, and he hastily swung at the woman in MERCENARY red. She spun out of its way, and her braided hair as well as her whip threatened to collide with him. He was forced to leap over her sweeping weapon, and his sword weighed him down as he barely escaped its circular path.

She steadied herself and brought the bulk of her whip back to her side. "Novice," she spat. She flung the weapon's thick body into the air and grabbed its end with her free hand.

He stabbed at his target, and she evaded the attack by leaping high above him. A briefly visible yellow streak continued to follow her unnatural movements. He hoisted his blade in an attempt to impale her as she fell back to the surface of the plate, but she landed safely behind him. She threw the middle of her whip over him and yanked both ends toward herself. He thwarted the attack by drawing his sword vertical and close to himself before she could tighten her weapon around him.

As she pulled back, he pushed forward. The recently sharpened blade tore into the thick braid and ripped it in two. He stumbled forward and nearly lost his balance. The weight of his sword allowed him to regain his center of gravity as he pivoted to face his opponent.

His grip on his weapon shifted and tightened. "Unless you have a backup plan, you're done," he spat.

Despite her broken weapon, Elena showed no fear. The pieces of the whip spun at her sides as she formed a stronger grip on both. Her arms rose above her head, and she yanked them down. The two pieces cracked in sync. A smile edged at the sides of her mouth. "You may have done me a favor, hero." The yellow essenia in her belt glowed brightly as she raced at him.

At the first hint of her attack, Cirrus swung his sword. He knew if he waited for her to come within range, he would be too late. His only hope was to anticipate her projected direction and aim for the future.

His blind attack resulted in contact. The hit came from one of the blade's flat sides, and it stripped her of her enhanced speed. She spun out of control and onto the plate's smooth surface.

"Impressive," she grunted. Her legs lifted into the air before she jerked them back down. The momentum brought her to her feet. "You're no imposter. You have MERCENARY training." She snapped the remnants of her whip again and stepped toward him. "A MERCENARY-soldier-turned-eco-terrorist? That's got to be a first."

Again, Elena leapt high into the air. As she passed above him, a shredded end of her whip smacked his face. A stinging pain shot through him as she landed. He rubbed his sore cheek against his shoulder. The araneid fabric scratched his sensitive skin, and he exhaled in frustration.

"Whatever damage your little firecracker might do won't make the morning news. That message your dead friend broadcast is already being written off as a hoax." Elena beamed. "You're the one who is done."

At that moment, Julie's homemade device detonated. The exploding canister's shrapnel cut through pipes and wires. Chemicals and vim mixed with flames. The flowing energy ignited in a hellish explosion that fed on itself. Fire raced through conduits that snaked throughout the building. Dust and an orange glow exploded from windows as the reactor erupted.

The wave of dirty heat swept Cirrus into the air. The cool darkness swallowed him as he was pushed beyond the plate. The red sliver of Rosa smiled in his direction, and the stars winked at him. Relief rushed through his body and mind as he relished the rapture that consumed his being.

87830471R00138

Made in the USA
Lexington, KY
01 May 2018